ISBN 0-9678285-0-3

Copyright © 2001 F.C. Erlanger

All rights reserved. Published by Lunchbox Press,
214 East College Street, Suite 201, Grapevine, TX 76051
www.lunchboxpress.com

Cover illustration by John Statema
Cover design by Jackson Creative
Interior design by Cusick Design

First printing, 2001
Printed in Canada

• •

Special thanks

To Phil, my wonderful husband and partner, whose undying support got me started and keeps me going.

To Bud Wall for sharing his creative genius, warped sense of humor and amazing characters with me.

To Phil Schaaf for introducing me to Lori and helping me get this book published.

To Lori Stacy, my publisher, and Nancy Laichas, my editor, for believing in the vision.

To John Statema, for his numerous creative contributions to this book.

To my family and many friends: Sandy, Brandt, Susan, Rob, Elliot, Dan, the Artist Way clan and countless others who helped and supported me along the way.

Para os meus pais, muito obrigado para os vossos sacraficios.

••

For Olivia

NETMAN
The Legend

By F.C. Erlanger
Illustrated by Bud Wall and John Statema

BASED ON THE ORIGINAL CONCEPT AND CHARACTERS CREATED BY BUD WALL

• •

Table of Contents

Prologue

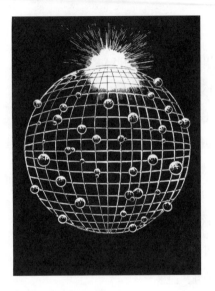

By the year 2111, the population on Thrae had soared to one billion people. The planet had become a powerhouse of unparalleled intelligence and technological capability, marked by its crowning achievement, the Net. A highly evolved version of Earth's old Web, the Net was no longer an archaic system of wires and cables hooked up to outdated computers around the globe that drained the environment. Instead, it had been transformed into an interactive virtual world that orbited in a parallel universe in space called Orion.

Home to half a billion Netpeople who maintained the systems that supported the vital operations back on Thrae, the Net thrived in Orion's energy-rich Trapezium Galaxy. Although situated in different universes, Thrae and the Net were linked by a secret gateway, called Cygnus X-5, a massive spinning black hole that allowed two-way communication and, for a brief hour once every eleven years, two-way traffic between the two worlds. This rare window for travel was called the Passage.

Thanks to its rich natural resources and the Net, Thrae had become the undisputed dominant order of the Black Galaxy and the envy of all other civilizations. But the Thraesians never anticipated the infinite riches the Net brought them, and thus naively built their technological Mecca without the proper safeguards. Little did they know that in the far reaches of the seemingly peaceful Trapezium Galaxy, on a bleak, arid planet called Dominion, dwelt the dark force of Orion, the Meta-hackers, an evil, juvenile civilization led by the notorious RedDwarf.

Thrae's peace-loving citizens feared that the recent stream of Viruses unleashed on the Net by the Meta-hackers could mean an end to their dream of an ideal society. Unfortunately, their fears were confirmed on a cool, windy morning, just days before the Passage.

One

THRAE

Weldon revved the engine of his BulletBike. A sleek, high-tech version of a turbo road bike, it had a retractable, low-angled shield that Weldon tucked his head under as he hugged the curves of the windy, cliffside road. The shield, a clear computer screen that monitored street conditions and anticipated problems, usually made driving hassle free. But lately, the planet Thrae had been hit by a wave of strange and unexplained computer malfunctions, and nothing was working quite right.

At first glance, Weldon looked like your average lanky fifteen-year-old, his radiant blue eyes barely visible under his unruly, wavy blond hair. However, he was anything but. Weldon was the pre-eminent computer genius of his time, and the Consortium, the bureaucratic ruling government of Thrae, was determined to use him for its own purposes. But Weldon was no fool. He knew that the Consortium's power had bred greed and corruption among its ranks, and that their short sightedness was largely to blame for the rampant spread of disease on the Net, Thrae's stellar planetary operations center. Now it was up to Weldon to protect the Netpeople, Thrae's working class, from the raging Viruses that threatened to destroy the Net.

Weldon had been dreading breaking the Meta-hacker news to the NetWatch Council all morning. Climbing the mountain road to Deadwood Lane, he took a deep breath and finally relaxed as the fresh scent of the eucalyptus forest below filled his lungs. He couldn't help but admire the beautiful city of Moravec. The capital of Thrae, Moravec was set in a valley surrounded on all sides by the majestic Rainer Mountains. The city glistened in the sun after having suffered a steady, two-week downpour of plasma rain, a by-product of the raging solar storms that swept the region every eleven years, bringing with them the mysterious Nauroras. These eerie glowing lights lit up the night skies with iridescent colors. Last evening, the rare Red Naurora had turned Thrae's night sky into a foreboding sea of flaming red, a warning that the powerful magnetic storm, DeathPing, was soon to hit.

As Weldon gazed down at the city, an AutoPorter whipped around the bend, heading right for him. His bike radar had failed to react. Immediately, he hit the emergency button on the throttle marked "turbo blast." A surge of power from the tailpipes shot him ten feet up and over the fishbowl-shaped glass AutoPorter packed with screaming six-year-olds. They whizzed by, mooning him as they passed. Weldon landed with a slight bounce and guided the bike back on the road. He shook his head at their antics, but couldn't really get angry. He hadn't been any better a driver when he was their age. With intelligent transport vehicles, you didn't have to be. The onboard computer did the driving for you, or at least that was the idea.

Weldon pulled up to the guardhouse at the foot of Deadwood Lane and waited to be checked in by Max, a colorful old NetWatch security guard who manned the high-voltage force field surrounding the grounds. Max had mentioned that in the last few days, flocks of unusual birds had been dive-bombing the grid, killing themselves en masse in strange attempts to penetrate it. Weldon knew it was an ominous sign. As the sun approached the peak of its eleven-year cycle, its accompanying storms threatened to wreak havoc on the electromagnetic structure of the Net, thus compromising Thrae's only security and leaving it completely vulnerable to a Meta-hacker attack.

A group of rowdy nine-year-olds pulled up behind him in a four-wheel-drive AutoTerrainPorter as Weldon waited. At fifteen, he already felt old. The Consortium had found that by the age of eighteen the human brain became clogged with dysfunctional personality behaviors that limited, and even inhibited, uncensored creative thinking, allowing judgment to rule in its place. Thus the Consortium decreed that all children of Thrae were to be tested at the age of two and, if deemed "gifted," recruited into the Osiris Tower, the Consortium's research-and-development think tank. There, operating as scientists, engineers, doctors, teachers, physicists and philosophers, they would pioneer solutions to any problems that plagued Thrae. The Osiris children were treated as dignitaries. They had free reign and could do no wrong. At eighteen, they would be retired to less important functions, like going to traditional school. Weldon knew that harnessing the brilliant young minds of kids was the secret to Thrae's success, but for some it came at a price.

"Late start this morning?" asked Max, scanning the silver NetWatch badge on Weldon's shirt.

"Yeah," said Weldon, exasperated. "I couldn't get out of the house. I got locked in."

"Can't trust those bloody home computers anymore, can we?" remarked Max. Weldon laughed as the gates opened and Max waved him through.

NetWatch was housed in an austere building nestled into the notorious

Deadwood Mountain. The only way to get to Thrae's Cybersecurity Headquarters was to climb the long, treacherously narrow road that wrapped around the mountain's edge. As he made his way up the road, Weldon often wondered why his father had designed such a peculiar building. Referred to by the locals as "The White House," it was a sleek, sterile structure made of an unusual stone that shimmered brilliantly in the light. Here, a renegade group of brilliant kids, hand picked by Weldon, worked in a shroud of secrecy, with complete autonomy from the Consortium, monitoring Virus activity on the Net.

Inside, Weldon stopped in the lobby to look up at the life-size portrait of his father hanging on the wall. Below it, a plaque read: "Tex Wall, 2030-2105. Founder of NetWatch, 2100."

Weldon's father had been one of the legendary settlers of Thrae. A famous computer scientist from Earth, Tex Wall had been determined to create a superior technological world on Thrae that would support—not drain—the natural resources of the land. His years of work culminated in the design and launch of the Net in 2067 and the advancement of artificial intelligence. Tex's dream of creating the first true "intelligent planet," where even a blade of grass could tell you if it needed water, had become a reality.

But the security measures enforced by the Consortium to protect the Net were inadequate, and the Meta-hackers, the dark force of Orion, soon exploited the gaps in its defenses by launching its "Army of Doom," the Viruses, to infiltrate it. Left with no choice, Weldon's father created NetWatch to protect the Net from the Virus infestation that threatened to destroy it.

Weldon barely remembered his parents now. He was only nine when both were killed after incubated Viruses multiplied out of control in their lab, attacking them. From then on, Weldon was raised by the elders of Thrae and groomed to take over his father's responsibilities. At twelve, he became head of NetWatch. By then, the "trickle" of Viruses seeping into the Net had become a steady stream, with no end in sight. At a loss for how to stop them, Weldon accidentally stumbled upon the answer one night in the dead of winter in 2108.

While sorting through his father's personal belongings in his old lab, Weldon discovered a book entitled *The Viral Mutants.* Sandwiched between its pages was an envelope marked "Weldon," containing what looked like a compact disc from 20th century earth. Fishing around, Weldon found an old computer system amongst the pile of junk in the room. He slipped the compact disc in and to his shock, his father, a short, stately man with Weldon's vibrant blue eyes, materialized before him and spoke.

"Weldon, what I am about to reveal can put you in great danger. It is top secret, and sought after by both the Meta-hackers, who suspect its existence, and the Consortium, who are threatened by the power of NetWatch." Weldon stood in shock. He couldn't believe what he was seeing.

"Buried under a false floor in the far corner of my lab is my secret project, Netman," continued the hologram. "I have programmed what exists of him to respond only to you. Please, take a look."

Weldon hesitated, afraid to take his eyes off his father for fear he might disappear. Slowly, he pulled himself away and walked over to a far corner of the room, not sure which "far corner" the hologram meant. He bounced on the boards with all his weight, but they were solid. He moved down and tried a few more. Nothing.

"Keep going," encouraged his father.

Shaking his head in disbelief, Weldon crossed the room to try his luck elsewhere. Suddenly he heard a board creak. He stopped, backed up two steps, and found an entire patch of creaky boards. Carefully prying them up, Weldon discovered a coffinlike titanium case lying beneath. He dragged it out and slowly popped the latches. He cracked the dusty lid and gasped. A half-built Cyborg stared back at him.

"I named him Netman," said his father proudly, walking closer. "I smuggled an earlier version of him into Thrae when I and the few thousand survivors fled Earth in the SpaceArks during the great blast of 2060.

He is the ultimate anti-virus Cyberwarrior, an artificial intelligent, lethal fighting machine, built to protect the Net by seeking and destroying any and all Viruses before they can spread their seed. He is the second—and final—generation of my work."

Mesmerized, Weldon looked over the Cyborg's sleek, cool design.

"I secretly launched the first-generation Netman when NetWatch, then a secret underground society, first observed viral activity in the Net. But after successfully completing a clean sweep of all Viruses. Netman suddenly expired due to a fatal code error," Tex said sadly. "He saved a great number of lives, that first one. Became something of a legend. The Consortium got wind of his existence and interrogated everyone, but learned nothing. We were all closely monitored after that. That is why you must be careful. This type of technology scares them. The Consortium preaches that in the wrong hands such a being could destroy Thrae, but it is their own power they fear for.

"Most of all, however," warned Tex, "beware of the Meta-hackers. They will stop at nothing to control the Net. They are in search of our secret gateway, Cygnus X-5, so they can gain entry into our Universe and strip Thrae of its rich resources."

Weldon discovered a secret compartment in the lining of the case and slid it open.

"Behind that panel," continued his father, "you will find my data files, journals, and detailed blueprints for Netman's completion, as well as plans for four future Cyberwarriors: Didgit, Ram, Krash and Burn. I refer to them as the CyberSquad: Netman's team of anti-Viruses. The plans call for brain mapping, which is strictly forbidden by the Consortium for fear of its potential threat to Thrae's security, but there is no other way."

Cyborgs, Weldon knew, had been outlawed long ago because of their susceptibility to viral infection. However, the idea of creating artificial-intelligent Cyborgs capable of independent thought and loaded with their master's intellect, personality and memories was a revolutionary concept.

"What you see is the culmination of my life's work," said Tex. "This

Netman is invincible; he is in a class of his own. Everything you need to know is in that case. I am entrusting him and the safety of the Net to you. Be careful."

Weldon reached longingly for his father's hand as the hologram faded, wishing desperately that he could hold it just one last time. But Weldon's hand passed through thin air.

His father smiled at him. Disappearing, his last words lingered in the air. "Good luck, son ... I'll be rooting for you."

It had taken them three years, but the NetWatch High Council— Weldon, Twiggy, Gopher, Skooter and Piper—had now nearly completed their work on Netman and the CyberSquad. All that remained was the brain mapping. Given the recent Meta-hacker news, Weldon knew it would have to happen tonight.

Riding up the glass encased escalator that hung off the side of the NetWatch building, Weldon glanced down at the river and saw that hundreds of people had already assembled at the Passage Gates. Hopeful wives, children and elderly parents were camped out, in anticipation of the long-awaited return of their friends and family members. In less than four days, the Netpeople would be coming home from their completed eleven-year tours of duty. Little did they know, thought Weldon as he stepped off the escalator, that the Meta-hackers were about to launch the biggest Cybergalactic ViralWar that the Net had ever seen.

Two

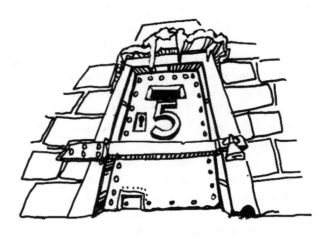

THE ABANDONED MINESHAFT

Entering NetWatch's huge, split-level loft, Weldon found the Cybersecurity Headquarters already buzzing with the Meta-hacker news. He walked briskly through the infamous Viral Holographic Hall of Fame, lined with the Net's Ten Most Wanted Viruses. Above each holograph, a computer board blinked with the status and whereabouts of each one. He was glad to see that all ten—BeastBomber, Mammoth, CowpaddyFly, NetTick, JunkFace, SiloKiller, Gargoyle, NeonSniper, HeadHunter and the most ruthless of all, BeelzeButt—were still on ice in the Net's VirusPrison.

He stepped up to the main floor. The place was on red alert. The

WhiteHats, fifty kids between the ages of eight and twelve who made up the NetWatch surveillance team, sat manning three-foot-long, flat-panel computer boards at circular work stations throughout the room. They were frantically running checks on various Netsystems. Weldon spotted Twiggy, a tall fourteen-year-old with long red hair, green eyes and a real stubborn streak, at the weather station. He regarded her as his partner and best friend even though they fought—a lot. She was bent over a computer board, correcting a weather station malfunction responsible for the two weeks of steady plasma rain. She looked up at him, smiling as he approached.

"Weldon. Nice to see you," she said sarcastically. "You missed the Consortium's little announcement in the emergency meeting this morning. Nothing important, just something about the Meta-hackers threatening to launch a Cybergalactic war against the Net and us being their only hope."

"I know," he said.

She smirked. It always irked her how he knew things before she did, and worse, was always so calm.

"Get everyone in the war room," he said, walking away. He stopped and looked back. "Nice trick altering the code on my home security system this morning," he said, smiling. "Wait until you see what your house has in store for you."

"I don't know what you're talking about," she said, trying to conceal her mischievous grin. He chuckled, walking away.

Weldon walked into the lab and found the ten-year-old twins, Skooter and Piper, in the glass-walled simulation room testing out new RocketBoards. The Boards morphed from small surfboard to snowboard to hovering street-luge racer in less than three seconds. Up on a gigantic video screen, Skooter surfed the teal blue waters off an exotic island paradise. Wearing his XK3 Netwatch and ZX1 Netshades, which simulated the virtual scene, he powered through killer fifty-foot curls on his RocketSurfboard, untouched. On another screen, Piper edged his RocketSnowboard down a virgin snow-covered mountain. He slid at eighty miles per hour straight down an extreme slope, his arms extended, screaming with joy. Weldon smiled. The twins were daredevils at heart, with insatiable appetites for extreme adventure that often got them in trouble.

Weldon flicked off the computer, killing their virtual world. Instantly, they stumbled and fell off the projection screen. Weldon laughed, but they didn't think it was funny.

"What are you doing?" yelled Skooter.

"I finally made it to level five!" whined Piper.

"Yeah, yeah. Come on, we've got a problem," said Weldon, waving them over.

Gopher, a studious eleven-year-old with more phobias than even he could count, walked in. "Weldon, everybody is assembled," he said, throwing the "kids," as he called them, a dirty look. "I've been trying to get those two off that simulator all morning."

"Hey Gopher," called Skooter, "I hear the Viruses have found a way to infiltrate Thrae and they're headed to your place during the Passage. Something about payback time."

"Very funny, like that's possible," said Gopher, nervously glancing at Weldon.

"Don't worry," reassured Weldon, leading him out, "I'll give you plenty of advance warning if they do."

They entered a small, enclosed amphitheater where all fifty WhiteHats were assembled, periodically checking their hand-held Netpilots for updates on Net crashes and station malfunctions. They stood as Weldon, Twiggy, Gopher, Skooter and Piper—the NetWatch High Council—entered. The five were an unlikely group, but the best in their respective fields. Twiggy was the incomparable Engineerdoc. She could fix any malfunction on the Net. Gopher was a renowned Virus expert. He could trace any Virus signature or fingerprint back to its host. He was also the leading expert in quantum physics and energy field manipulation. Skooter and Piper, the extreme adventure junkies, were ingenious inventors. They had developed the most sought-after weapons and toys in the galaxy. Lastly,

Weldon was the brilliant tactical strategist, a fearless renegade and a born leader. Like his father, he was determined to protect the Net and its Netpeople, whom the Consortium increasingly treated as dispensable as the years passed and their coffers filled.

Weldon took his place at center stage in front of a massive hundred-foot-long screen as the other four took their seats in the first row behind their consoles. On Weldon's cue, Scooter dimmed the lights and Gopher activated the hologram. A three-dimensional image of the Net appeared behind Weldon. The Net resembled Saturn, the sixth planet in Earth's solar system, but with hundreds of crisscrossing rings around it, forming a floating weblike lattice over Alpha Centauri, the raging sun that rotated within it, fueling it with energy. Interspersed throughout the Net were over fifty moons of every shape and size, each home to various Netpeople who worked the respective Net operations based on their moon. The interconnecting strands of the Net between the moons, called HighBand, made up the information superhighway that allowed data to travel beyond the speed of light from moon to moon and finally, through the Cygnus X-5 gateway back to Thrae.

Weldon motioned for silence. "As you know, the Meta-hackers are threatening to launch a Cybergalactic war against the Net if we don't give them the gateway coordinates that lead to our Aries Universe.

"In four days, the Net and Thrae will rotate into perfect alignment with that gateway, the Cygnus X-5 black hole, opening a one-hour window for us to transport back to Thrae those Netpeople who have completed their tours of duty and send in reinforcements.

"During this window," Weldon continued, " we are extremely vulnerable to attack. This alignment historically weakens the Net's communication and defense system. It is this unstable environment that the Meta-hackers are counting on to use as a shield to strike in force.

"The key objective now is to monitor every square inch of the Net and Thrae for any clues of malfunctions that somehow may be linked to their plot so we can be prepared to stop them. It is critical we do everything in our power to ensure the Netpeoples' safe return. If the Meta-hackers' army of Viruses succeeds in infiltrating the Net, we will be unable to protect the Netpeople and Thrae will be in danger of falling under their control. I am counting on each of you to work around the clock. We don't have much time. Gopher is going to brief you on the five most likely Viruses in the wild who could be behind this, and who have enough support to lead a Cybergalactic war."

Gopher took the stage as five pictures flashed on the screen. They were a terrifying bunch, with gruesome features and horrible deformities. He pointed to each as he read the names aloud: "MonkeyDropper, ChickenChoker, JunkModemPole, Piranus and lastly, the Great Wormagon."

He pointed back to the first picture. "The MonkeyDropper lives in the jungles of the Net, camouflaging himself as a tree, hiding his grotesque head and peering eyes in its bushy top. His weapons are the small poisonous monkey, nesting in his dense branches. Once he nears his victim, he drops monkeys by the hundreds who swarm all over their prey. If bitten by one, you die a slow, painful death. The monkeys multiply with the taste of blood. Only known defense: K4, a rare poisonous gas, which has to be handled carefully or it will kill you."

He moved his pointer to the next picture. "The ChickenChoker is a mutated chicken with numerous arms capable of reaching out ten feet in all directions. He can crush you in his iron grip in seconds. He travels the wooded areas of the Net. Only known defense: fire."

Gopher pointed down to the next two. "JunkModemPole and Piranus are the craftiest of the five. They are both water-dwelling Viruses. One stalks the LowBand Cyberrivers while the other travels the Cyberwaters of HighBand." He tapped the picture of the Great Wormagon. "And we can't discount the Great Wormagon, the keeper of BeelzeButt's VirusColony. Part lizard, part worm, he might be dumb, but he's deadly."

As Gopher continued, Weldon and Twiggy slipped out. "We have to launch him," Weldon said, heading down the hall to his office.

"Who?" asked Twiggy, following.

"Netman."

"But we haven't found a retrieval system yet. VC6 is a one-way worm-hole. We send them down to the Net and we'll never get them back. The MessageLogs will be the only way we can communicate with them. And even that's not secure."

"We don't have a choice," argued Weldon. "He's our only hope. We have to execute the brain-mapping transfer tonight."

"Our brain-mapping technique has barely been tested," said Twiggy. "We don't know what giving a Cyborg completely independent thought, and carbon copies of our brains, including our personality traits—a scary thought, I might add—will mean in battle."

"Our reasoning will only help them," reassured Weldon. "It will be like we're there."

"Great," said Twiggy, as Weldon entered his office. "They're doomed."

* * *

At midnight, Twiggy, Gopher, Skooter and Piper met Weldon in his office.

Weldon opened up the small cabinet against his wall and punched his private code into the keypad. Immediately, a wall slid back, revealing a hidden passageway that led to a long set of stairs.

On the landing below stood a table with five clear glass bowls lined in a row, each filled with a rainbow-colored liquid. The five removed the oblong badges that Thrae's citizens were required to wear at all times. The badge, which transmitted pertinent personal information to all computer devices, made life hassle-free. Like a butler, it opened doors, ordered gro-ceries and even knew when a transporter needed fixing. But its real pur-pose was to enable the Consortium to constantly monitor the whereabouts of its citizens. The group plopped their badges into the bowls. The loca-tion-altering solution tricked the Consortium's computer systems into believing the badges were still on them and registered them walking around a selected decoy location.

"There, that should hold them," said Weldon, leading on. "Watch your step."

They descended into the dank, long-abandoned mineshaft, each grabbing a laser torch from the wall to illuminate the way. The shaft, which Weldon had learned of in his father's journal, ran below NetWatch and through the belly of Deadwood Mountain. Gopher shivered from the cold as he trailed the group down the dark, eerie mine shaft. Goosebumps ran up his spine. A hundred yards down, at the far end of the dusty mine shaft, they stopped in front of five heavily bolted doors.

Weldon stepped down to the last, marked No. 5, and slowly unlocked it. It was common knowledge that Tex Wall had built two wormholes to facilitate travel to Cygnus X-5. One was on Thrae and the other on the Net, commonly referred to as the Passage Gates. But only Weldon knew there was a third, Room No. 5.

Weldon and the others entered the dimly lit room. It was empty except for the five metal brain-drain contraptions against the far wall that remotely resembled barber's chairs but with strange electronic apparatus protruding from all sides. On each seat was a clear helmet pulsating with a current of violet light from the many wires and electrodes running through it.

"In a few minutes," Weldon said, "we will begin brain-mapping. Everything we know, everything we have experienced, and even everything we fear, will be fed into Netman and the CyberSquad. If any of them are ever captured, they can easily be traced back to us and we will be killed either by the Meta-hackers, or the Consortium for treason." He paused, looking at them squarely. "Are you ready to launch Netman and the CyberSquad into the Net?"

They nodded, recognizing the gravity of what they were about to do. "Mantor," called Weldon.

From behind a black curtain, a Cyborg with a shaved head and piercing green eyes appeared. He was dressed in a burnished orange ornamental robe wrapped tightly around his body, with its draping sleeves all but covering his deformed hands. His waist was cinched with a brilliant yellow belt, adorned with hundreds of shimmering gemstones that seemed to encase him in a field of energy as he walked. Mantor was the only one of his kind, developed by Weldon specifically to help guard and launch Netman. He bowed his head, greeting them.

"Start the download," Weldon instructed.

Responding, "Yes, master," Mantor walked to the far wall and opened a glass panel illuminated with multicolored lights. He pressed a triangular red button. The wall behind the chairs vanished, revealing five identical contraptions positioned back-to-back with the other chairs. Strapped into them were five hooded Cyborgs: Netman and the CyberSquad. Weldon nodded silently for everyone to take their places.

Weldon climbed into the chair to the far right behind the Cyborg marked "Netman." He was the tallest, almost seven feet, with a thin, humanlike body covered in green silicon skin, and unusually long, flat feet that balanced out his oversized head. Weldon strapped on his helmet and slipped his feet into the restraints. Twiggy took the chair next to Weldon behind the Cyborg marked "Didgit." Didgit was almost identical to Netman, but slightly smaller in size. Twiggy took a deep breath as she fastened her helmet, hoping they were doing the right thing. Gopher reluctantly took the chair next to Didgit behind the Cyborg marked "Ram." Aptly named, his body resembled that of a powerful, upright Ram. The tips of his multicolored horns protruded from special holes on the sides of his enormous hood. Gopher nervously slipped on the helmet, wondering if this were really safe. Piper jumped into the chair next to Gopher behind the Cyborg marked "Krash." He resembled a stocky eight-year-old kid, no more than four feet tall, with a bright yellow silicon body and short, orange trunklike legs with ski-boot-shaped feet. Piper quickly threw on the helmet and adjusted the hand restraints. Skooter gave "Burn" a friendly swat on the head and plopped into the last chair behind him. Krash and Burn were identical twins, although Skooter and Piper failed to see the resemblance.

As Skooter quickly strapped in, he leaned forward to Gopher, who was already perspiring, and said, "Hey, we never got around to testing your chair. So if you feel like your brain is on fire, it could be. Good luck!"

Weldon winked reassuringly at Gopher, who was quickly reconsidering. Weldon gave the signal to Mantor. Everyone slipped on their eyeshields and braced themselves for the jolt.

Mantor flipped the power switch on the wall and the NetWatch helmets surged with a blinding white light that scanned and simultaneously sucked the genetic code from their brains and pumped it into the craniums of the Cyborgs immediately behind them. In seven minutes, the brain-mapping was complete. Mantor killed the switch and ran vitals on Weldon and the others. Satisfied with the results, he flicked on a yellow light, replenishing and nourishing the NetWatch Council's brains with energy, and the five began to stir from their hypnotic state. Mantor slowly turned down the dial until the light was extinguished, and brought the group back to consciousness.

"Everything we know," said Weldon, "everything we are, they now are."

Twiggy shook her head, removing her restraints. "I hope that's a plus."

"Well, maybe not for Didgit," said Weldon.

"Very funny," said Twiggy, shoving him. Suddenly the lights flickered.

"We'd better activate them before we run into transmission problems," warned Weldon. He walked across the room and threw open the curtain Mantor had entered through, revealing a master Cyberspace command center behind it, complete with a 30-foot computer board that ran the length and height of the wall. They each took their assigned seats at their stations.

"Twiggy, run vitals on Netman and the CyberSquad and prepare resuscitation," Weldon ordered. "Gopher, check the travel conditions in the VC6 black hole. Make sure there is no turbulence between here and its connecting point into the Cygnus X-5. Piper and Skooter, initialize the Rocket capsules and make sure all systems are go."

"Mantor," called Weldon, "hook up communication links between NetWatch and the NetRockets. I want to monitor them every step of the way. I'll program the landing coordinates for their Net entry. Commence launch."

Piper and Scooter started the initialization. Five bright beams of light encapsulated Netman and each of the CyberSquad members, morphing their chairs into long, sleek NetRockets.

Mantor pulled the red lever under the glass case on the center console, announcing, "Sixty seconds to launch."

Suddenly, a deafening alarm sounded throughout the building. "That's a Code Five!" yelled Twiggy.

"Can't be!" shouted Weldon, checking the NetWatch core system.

"I can't believe it," said Gopher, examining the code. "A Virus has infiltrated the NetWatch security sector. They're attacking our communication links with the Net."

"That's not all," said Twiggy, scrolling through the defense log. "The NetWatch Firewall has been activated. It's shutting down all our systems." Twiggy looked at Weldon. "We're going dark."

Just then, Room No. 5 began to shake and break apart.

Piper yelled, "The Rockets are launching!"

"I can't stop them!" shouted Mantor, frantically working the controls.

Weldon watched in horror as the computer board slid back, revealing the mouth of the turbulent VC6 black hole, known as the VC6, violently churning behind it. Tornadolike winds filled the room.

Twiggy desperately tugged at Weldon as the others ran to safety. "Come on! We've got to get out!"

Weldon pulled away. "No! I have to stop the launch. The coordinates aren't set. They'll be lost!"

"There's nothing you can do now!" screamed Twiggy, barely hanging on as the force of the winds threatened to suck them into Cyberspace. "You'll die!"

The NetRockets turned into position, facing west for entry into VC6.

The computer stations lowered into the floor to clear the way.

"It's too late!" yelled Twiggy. The NetRockets disengaged. At the last second, Weldon grabbed Twiggy and bolted out the door as the Rockets roared into the black hole's stormy abyss. Weldon prayed that his father's journal was right and VC6 fed directly into the Cygnus X-5 black hole, otherwise Netman and the CyberSquad would be lost forever.

Suddenly, Door No. 5 slammed shut. As quickly as it started, it was over. Weldon ran back and flung open the door. They were gone.

"We have to find them!" called Weldon, running for the stairs with the others close behind.

Reaching the main floor, the five were bombarded with frantic WhiteHats reporting on Thrae's red-alert status. Weldon stopped short when he saw the central alert board flooded with red lights indicating malfunctions all over Thrae.

"The power and water service has been shut down," reported one. "It's a blackout. We're running on backup generators."

"All electronic communications are down," announced another. "We can't log on to our substations."

Weldon jumped on the central computer and tried to get the system up and running. He yelled to Twiggy, "What's the status of the other sectors?"

Frantically searching the system she yelled back, "Everything else is checking out. Maybe it's just a storm surge that knocked out some of the key servers."

Piper yelled from a console across the room, "No, the storm sector in Cygnus is quiet."

"I don't like it," said Weldon. "Where's the Virus?"

"I can't find a Virus signature. It must be a Polymorpher," called out Gopher.

"Skooter, shut down all B and C systems on Thrae," ordered Weldon. "We're on red alert!"

Weldon switched over to an auxiliary system, trying in vain to make contact with the NetRockets, but the transmission was dead. Weldon refused to believe that he might have just thrown away his father's life's work.

Suddenly the large board came alive with images of seven white-haired, aristocratic men in long blue robes, seated at a long table. It was the Consortium. The leader announced to Weldon, "We have a red alert. Our basic services are failing. We have flooding in the canals, the power has been shut off and we have no electronic interplanetary communications. Have you detected any Viral activity?"

"Yes, but we haven't been able to pinpoint their exact location or identity," said Weldon.

The leader gravely continued. "Our talks broke down with the Meta-hackers. They have officially declared war on the Net. They will stop at nothing to expand their power base into our Aries universe. If they succeed—" The transmission went dead.

Twiggy and Weldon whipped around, shocked to see a young, grotesque figure with oozing lesions on the left side of his deformed humanlike face covering all the computer screens.

The deadly voice warned, "Beware of the RedDwarf, Weldon! You're little team is not a match for me. Let the games begin!!!"

The main floor went black.

Three

VIRUSPRISON

Isolated in the far reaches of the Net's sector 8 was the dark FornaxMoon, nicknamed "the Underground." Fornax's unusual position on the Net made sunlight impossible. The moon's single inhabited city, Methuselah, was settled only to house the infamous VirusPrison, where all the Net's captured Viruses were incarcerated. Still others lurked on its cold, damp and dirty streets. The Viruses prowled amidst the junk and burned-out transporters from VirusGang wars and system crashes that littered vacant lots and abandoned parks. Old, rundown buildings were infested with VirusMites that got into everything—clothes, beds, furniture, hair—and spread like wildfire, causing a telltale red, itchy rash to spread all over the faces, hands and arms of the unfortunate Netpeople stationed on Fornax. The rash itself oozed a greenish-brown pus that gave off the foul odor of rotting flesh, making the already rank air even more putrid.

Viruses loved to hide out in Methuselah because no one patrolled its streets. They were too afraid. The Netpeople serving their tour in the Underground were usually Thrae's poorest, with little money or influence to secure better assignments. They took the only jobs available, working at the Prison as guards or administrators. These were the most dangerous jobs on the Net.

The Prison sat high atop the cliffs of Serpent Mountain, surrounded by a moat of vile, bubbling hot springs that spurted from the ground. An invisible, domelike magnetic force field covered the Prison, keeping out the hundreds of swarming VirusVultures, who, intent on freeing their evil masters within, continually circled above.

Inside, the guards grew uneasy as the sun storms intensified and systems failed. They feared that with the Passage only three days away, the Meta-hackers could strike at any hour. The Consortium had warned them that the Prison could be the first target.

Froug stood at his post in the depths of the dim catacombs, preparing to start roll call. He was an older guard with graying hair and a slow, deliberate walk. He moved through the catacombs, his fire torch in hand. Light agitated the Viruses, so their cages were always kept pitch black. The dim lanterns on the corridor walls barely lit his path.

But tonight the prisoners were restless anyway. The deadly Viruses violently shook their cell bars, trying to intimidate Froug as he walked down the corridor. Some cells held two and three Viruses within a ten-by-six-foot space. Occasionally mixed in with them was a Virus mutation known as a Vermin. Viruses and Vermin were a terrifying sight. Some resembled deformed animals and evil toys, while others looked like deadly contraptions or even wicked humans. But underneath, they were all highly sophisticated killing machines—mutated, hideous breeds of Cyborgs.

Froug glanced nervously at a passing cage, as one Virus ripped into his Vermin cellmate. He knew mixing Viruses and Vermin together was a dangerous practice. Vermin considered themselves the true outlaws of the Net. They abhorred the rules of the VirusColony and considered Viruses nothing more than sellouts and puppets of the greedy Meta-hackers. Viruses, on the other hand, considered Vermin reckless, stupid and inferior creatures whose random and disorganized strikes against the Net made them more of a nuisance than a true threat to power. Often they'd tear each other apart, leaving the guards to clean up and contain the spread of their deadly seed.

But the guards had no choice. The Prison couldn't keep up with the number of deadly Viruses routinely apprehended in the far reaches of the Net. And like deadly radioactive waste, they couldn't be destroyed, only contained. With the Prison beyond maximum capacity, systems were beginning to show signs of weakness, and guards were now outnumbered ten to one.

Froug stopped and carefully checked the nameplate on the Prison cage before starting the roll call. "HogHead!" he shouted, thrusting his torch through the bars. A snorting, piglike creature with two long tusks sticking out from the sides of its oozing snout ran back as the torch came near. Fire was one of the few things Viruses feared because it altered their seed, which lived in the soft plasma center of their hearts. Froug continued down the aisle. "MoonRat!" he called. An enormous rodent with a thick, scaly tail, razor-sharp teeth and hairy, pockmarked skin scurried to the far corner as the torch lit up the cage.

Froug often thought about whether he would have volunteered to serve on the Net for the eleven-year tour of duty—the equivalent of forty-four years on Thrae—if he had known about the time warp. He had believed their promises: that the Consortium would protect him, that infestation was impossible, and that he would come home to reap the financial rewards of having served Thrae. But experience had shown him otherwise. He hoped for the best now that his turn to go home was approaching.

A tall, frightening marionette, with hypnotic black eyes and a long, pointy beak stood defiantly at the cage bars. The nameplate read: "The Puppet." "Back!" Froug yelled, as he nervously thrust the torch at him. It stood firmly, staring defiantly at Froug. Then, leaning forward, the Puppet whispered, "It won't be long now." A cold shiver ran up Froug's back.

The head guard, Asylum, suddenly appeared walking briskly down the hall toward Froug. "I need you down in DeepFreeze," he called. "We have a problem." Froug handed his torch to a passing guard and followed Asylum through the maze of catacombs. Door after door took them deeper into the vilest sectors of the Prison. Hundreds of strange, deformed and deadly Viruses lashed out as they passed their cages. At times like these Froug wondered how he and his son, Croix, had managed to live all these years in the Underground and escape infection. He considered himself lucky. He often thought of his wife, who hadn't been as fortunate.

Finally, they reached a 20-foot-high, bolted steel door marked "DeepFreeze." Two huge guards stepped aside as Asylum punched in his code. The door slowly slid open, releasing a cloud of chilling vapors into the anteroom, engulfing the two of them as they disappeared into the circular glass tunnel. The tunnel throbbed with a strange hum as purple iridescent beams pulsated across it, creating a grid of light that scanned their bodies as they walked through. Froug's scan showed nothing but his skeletal structure, whereas Asylum's revealed a small pocket of red maggots slithering inside his heart—the mark of Virus infestation. Scientific advances had enabled the Netpeople to arrest the spread of the seed, allowing thousands to live with infestation for a few years before it ultimately killed them.

Perched at the end of the tunnel were treacherous, spiraling stairs, carved into the west wall of a steep abyss that plummeted to the DeepFreeze chamber below. Froug followed, descending slowly, his stomach knotting up with each step as they neared the bottom and he saw the door. Blinking in red letters on an electronic signpost ahead were the words "Warning! Entering DeepFreeze ... a living graveyard of the deadliest and most virulent strains."

Asylum passed his hand over a blue screen monitor and the giant door slid open. Froug prepared himself as they entered the cavernous room. It was a cool 40 degrees below zero. He shivered as the bitter cold air filled his lungs. It didn't matter how many times he entered DeepFreeze, he always looked away. The sight of hundreds of the Net's most lethal and ruthless Viruses frozen alive, dangling from the ceiling inside clear cylindrical ice casings, still made his skin crawl. Suspended from long support cables, they hung like Christmas tree ornaments just eight feet off the ground. Each cable connected to its own security-monitoring device below. The tall box's computer screens glowed with the name, number and pertinent statistics of each of the Viruses. Armed guards strolled silently up and down the aisles.

Asylum abruptly stopped in front of a monitor flashing: "BEELZEBUTT, VR666." The screen read:

WARNING! Life-sucking amphibian Virus! Lives in swampy pools, lakes or streams. Enormous, extended rumplike cranium holds gelatinous poisonous fluid which, when sprayed, is deadly on contact. Emits putrid odor. No known weaknesses. Reputed Leader of the VirusColony.

Everyone knew of BeelzeButt. He was the founder of the VirusColony, a secret Virus fraternity only the powerful and ruthless could join. The most dangerous Virus strains were represented among its ranks. It had taken NetWatch years to finally get BeelzeButt behind bars and bring down the powerfully organized Colony.

"See what you can do," said Asylum, pointing to BeelzeButt's security monitor. "It's been acting up all day."

Froug opened the control panel and immediately saw the problem. "It's nothing," he said, removing the burned-out energy circuit.

Across the floor, guards worked diligently to repair three other malfunctioning monitors. Asylum watched, worried. "I don't like it."

"Don't worry," Froug reassured. "The Passage will be over in four days."

"It won't be soon enough," Asylum muttered back.

Froug replaced the dead circuit with a new one. He couldn't deny it; he felt it, too. The Passage came only once every eleven years, but legend warned that it awakened the evil forces of the Universe. Understandably, everyone got uneasy as the Passage grew nearer and things "mysteriously" malfunctioned.

"There, that should do it," said Froug, closing up the box.

"What do you think? Will it be a quiet one?" asked Asylum.

Froug forced a laugh. "I hope so. I'm finally going home."

Asylum looked out at the sea of bodies. "You're lucky," he said. "For some of us, this is home," he added, walking away.

Froug busily packed up his small tools. Above, a drop of water ominously formed undetected on BeelzeButt's ice casing. It slid slowly down the figure's hideous face and splashed to the ground, just missing Froug as he turned and walked away.

Four

A VAGABOND'S PROPHECY

The following day, a fleet of brightly colored IMX transporters—high-speed Cyberspaceships—zoomed into the NorthCity Portal. These moon entrances were high-tech docking stations that could only be accessed by traveling through HighBand down into the dangerous, Virus-infected LowBand region, notorious for its treacherous terrain.

Froug and his eleven-year-old son, Croix, quickly exited the black IMX transporter. They were late for the Passage Ceremony. The noisy streets of NorthCity, the capital of Kappa and base of operations for the Net's ruling government, were crammed with joyous Netpeople exiting the massive ships arriving from all quadrants of the Net. Although Netpeople were not permitted Intermoon travel for safety and security reasons, on this one special day every eleven years, all were allowed to travel to participate in the Passage Ceremony and trade in the marketplace.

Froug walked hurriedly through the crowded street pulling Croix behind him. The thin, timid black-haired boy stared at his surroundings in awe. Croix had often dreamed of what life was like outside the dark, oppressive and dangerous streets of the Underground, but he couldn't believe his eyes. The NorthCity was warm and sunny, overgrown with exotic plants. Towering metallic buildings pierced the sky, hovering over the stately structures that lined the streets.

"Hurry, we're late," Froug said anxiously.

"You didn't tell me it would be like this," said Croix, amazed.

"You haven't seen anything yet."

Ten minutes later, Froug and Croix arrived at the decorated doors of the WarriorDome, a renowned outdoor arena constructed to pay tribute to the historical Cyberwarriors of their Orion Universe.

"Now, you remember what I said?"

"Bow, be silent and don't cry out," recited Croix.

"Right," confirmed Froug. "And enjoy yourself."

"Right," Croix responded with a hint of sarcasm.

As they entered the magnificent structure, Croix began to understand the significance of what was about to happen. The hallowed hall was painted with vibrant colors that depicted scenes from famous Virus fights held in the arena. Captured Viruses were originally pitted against Vermin in a fight to the death for all Netpeople to enjoy. It was an early Net tradition that the Consortium quickly outlawed after splattered VirusSeed flew into the audience, infecting hundreds.

Croix couldn't take his eyes off the royal statues of former NetRulers and infamous Anatares Cyberwarriors that lined the hall. He marveled at the floating cases beside them filled with magic gems, old anti-Virus weaponry and historical artifacts, some preceding the founding of the Net. He had never seen a shrine celebrating bravery and leadership.

Froug led Croix through the packed amphitheater down to the crowded field. Croix was astounded at the incredible diversity of Netpeople that had gathered. It was as if they were all from different worlds.

"Look at them all," he marveled.

"There are more than fifty moons," said Froug. "Each one has its own distinct culture and unique expertise. We celebrate our differences here. You'll see."

Once they reached the stage, they were escorted to a special cordoned-off section. As the Great Rhinose, the NetRuler, took the Grand Stage, a ceremonial vibration was sounded and all obediently sat down.

The Great Rhinose, a stocky, upright Rhinoceros who took himself way too seriously, said with hooves outstretched, "Welcome, Netpeople, to the opening of the fourth Imperial Ceremonies." He pointed to those in Croix's section, "We are here to honor these Netpeople who have completed their tour of duty on the Net and are now going home to glorious Thrae." The crowd applauded. Croix looked up at his father, beaming with excitement.

Rhinose dramatically swept his hoof across the vast crowd and continued, "You represent the amazing diversity of Net moons that make up the fabric of this technological Mecca. Without your hard work, the Net and Thrae's glorious kingdom would cease to exist." Croix and Froug joined the others in thunderous applause.

"Join me in the marketplace after the Purification Procession," he beckoned, "to behold each moon's exhibit, showcasing their land's great culture, customs and Net operations. Let us celebrate and honor our individual contributions to this collective force that has given birth to the Net. We alone have created it and it is up to us to protect it from the forces of evil, lest we end up like the infected," he said, pointing to the thousands of sickly looking Netpeople barricaded in the distance. Croix looked back sadly, recognizing many from the Underground and knowing well their life of shame and isolation.

The Great Rhinose continued. "They will unfortunately be banished to the Net forever. Don't let that be you! Let us celebrate the Passage of the Chosen and our time to come. May the Imperial Ceremonies begin!" Loud, vibrantly colored explosions filled the sky over the cheering crowd.

Moments later, the Chosen were escorted out, single file, to the nearby holy Purification stream. Croix, the only kid in the group, was instructed to go first. He stepped barefoot into the cold, shallow water and slowly waded along the glistening sandy bottom until he reached the High Priest, who stood on stone pilings above the river's edge. Croix climbed carefully up the makeshift rock steps and knelt nervously before him. The High Priest dipped his scepter into the water below. Croix bowed and extended his left hand. He felt the drops of the magic water land on the crown of his head. "You, my child, are free," pronounced the High Priest. "Go in peace to love and serve your kingdom." He pulled a burning branding rod out of a hot ash-filled urn and lightly seared the letter "C" on the back of Croix's left hand just below his tattooed name, thereby christening him a "Chosen One." Croix flinched at the touch of the burning metal, biting down hard on his lip to stop himself from crying out in pain. He stood and dutifully responded, "May the great Universe bless and protect the Netpeople." He stepped down as his father ascended for his blessing.

Once all had received their rites, the High Priest addressed the group. "You have fulfilled your destiny here. It is time to reap the rewards of your dutiful labor. Thrae awaits you. Return here in three days to journey through the Passage Gates at midnight into the kingdom of Thrae. Bring nothing and pass quickly, for the Gates will not stay open long."

The High Priest turned to the "Infected Ones" now gathered on the other side of the river. "You have not been forgotten. Come and drink from the cup. The blessed ViralSerum will ease your pain and slow the spread of your infection." As they slowly climbed the steps, he held the cup to their lips. After each one drank from the cup, he seared the letter X, the universal symbol for the infected, on the backs of their right hands.

Croix walked a bit lighter on his feet knowing that the procession was behind him. He had heard about the marketplace and the displays of wares from all around the Net, but he couldn't believe his eyes as he followed his father through the packed streets. A colorful bazaar had taken over the town attracting every unusual and eccentric type of NetCreature, all of them busily trading their wares with others from distant lands.

Froug pointed to a booth on the left. "That's the GreenMarb Moon. They call it the ElectronicForest because it resembles a lush forest, but when you examine its trees, grass and rocks, you discover they are actually made up of small automatrons. It's the home of the PageBoys, who maintain all the Net's WebPages."

Croix watched the elflike boys run around, repairing the virtual, interactive promotional film depicting life in the ElectronicForest. Froug pointed to another booth on the right. "That's Volan CF1, better known as the Matrix, home to all NetServers. It's the most guarded moon on all of the Net." Croix nodded, intrigued by the NetServer's enormous gelatinous heads barely supported by their tiny legs. They were odd but regal-looking creatures.

"They are the geniuses of the Net," continued Froug, "who hold all knowledge and information. Without them, we are nothing." Croix smiled, noting that even the small baby Servers looked noble and intellectual.

"What's that?" asked Croix, pointing to a stately booth just ahead.

"That's RedMarb V240. They call it Cray, headquarters of the Net's entire communication fleet. It's master control, where all Thrae information requests are processed and dispatched. Cray is home to the Routers, who direct traffic across the Net, to the BigEndians who command the transporters across HighBand and, of course, to the Packets, who carry the bits of information."

Croix marveled at the officious crowd inside the booth. "I wish we could travel to all these moons," he said. "They're nothing like the Underground. Why is our moon so dark and ugly and filled with infected Netpeople, when everyone else lives in beautiful cities?"

"Let's not linger on the past," Froug said, encouragingly. "We're going home."

"But why did we have to live there, when we weren't infected?"

"Someday you'll understand."

"Why not now?" asked Croix.

Sitting him down in a quiet patch of shade, Froug finally relented and revealed what he had hidden for years. "Your mother and I used to live in the ElectronicForest." Croix looked up, confused. "It was a beautiful place," Froug continued, "but one day there was a Viral outbreak, and she was infected." Croix sat stunned.

"She was pregnant with you at the time. When they heard she was sick they shipped us out immediately to the Underground. In those days, people were afraid to be around anyone infected. Today, we know that with treatment, infection can be contained and life prolonged. They gave me the option to stay in the ElectronicForest. But I could never leave you and your mother."

"After your birth, as you know, she died. They said it was a miracle she had the strength to deliver you. Afterward, I tried very hard to get us out. I petitioned the Consortium to hear our case and let us move back to the ElectronicForest, but we were denied. They said it was only a matter of time before you became sick and the Virus grew within you." A shudder ran up Croix's spine. "Don't worry," reassured Froug. "It hasn't and it won't." Croix suddenly felt responsible for their miserable lives.

"Some say that the healthy offspring of an infected one is a good omen, that they are blessed with magical powers," said Froug encouragingly. Croix forced a smile, but didn't believe it.

"That's all in the past now," said Froug, wrapping his arm around his son. "We're starting a new life. You can be anything you want on Thrae. Come," he said, pulling him up. "We can't change the past, but we can enjoy the present and look forward to our future. Now, let's go explore and enjoy the rest of our day." Croix nodded, hiding his concern.

They turned a corner minutes later and stumbled into a booth marked

"Katia, The Magic Sphere." Froug stopped short. "I can't believe it! I've been waiting to get you one of these since you were born."

"What?" asked Croix.

"Katia is known for its gem and crystal mines," explained Froug. "Their gems have magic powers that protect against evil."

Froug slipped off his ruby ring, his only valuable possession. "Stay here." Croix grabbed his hand. "Father, no! Mother gave that to you."

"It's just a ring, Croix. My memories of her are here," he said, pointing to his heart. "No one can ever take that away. Besides," he said, ruffling Croix's hair, "I know she'd want you to have one."

As he watched his dad get into the long line, Croix thought how lucky he was to have him for a father. Froug was the most honorable and loving person he had ever met. He was Croix's hero.

While waiting, Croix wandered over to a nearby booth marked, "Vajra, Moon of Warriors." Drawn to a collection of swords used by the ancient Anatares warriors who guarded the Orion universe against Viral Mutants long before the Net, Croix reached down and ran his fingers across the exotic display of weaponry. Across the booth, a decrepit female Vagabond in a hooded cape watched Croix keenly, her eyes carefully following his hand as he ran it along the swords. Suddenly, one of the blades cut his finger. Embarrassed, he quickly stuffed his bloodied hand into his pocket.

Casting a doubtful eye on Croix, the sword merchant approached and asked sternly, "Do you have a trade?"

"How much are they?" stuttered Croix, pretending he might.

"Hah!" scoffed the merchant. "More than you could ever afford."

Croix looked down in shame at his tattered clothes and dirty, hole-riddled shoes. He should have known better. He desperately wanted to fit in, but was afraid he never would. The Vagabond watched Croix get swallowed up by the crowd as others pushed their way forward. She quickly pulled a blinding, thirty-carat aqua-blue crystal from her pocket. Leaning forward, she extended her hand toward the merchant and asked, "What will you give me?"

Eyes wide, he snatched the precious stone and swept his hand over his entire collection, eagerly saying, "Pick one, my lady." She grabbed the bloodied sword and set off through the crowd.

Croix kicked the dirt beneath his feet as he watched his father slowly edge closer to the front of the line. Suddenly, a cold, clammy hand fell on his neck. He turned, jumping at the sight of the deformed face of the Vagabond in front of him.

"I don't have anything," he stuttered, trying to hide his disgust at her wart-infested face.

"But I do," she said, pulling the glistening sword from under her cape and offering it to him. He was shocked. "Please," she urged. "It's a gift."

He hesitated. Then, slowly, he extended his hand and took it. She leaned in close, cupping her hand around his ear, and whispered "They will call you the Scorpion Prince. You are weak, but He will make you strong. Be prepared, for destiny will soon call."

A hand suddenly slapped him on the back. Croix jumped, scared out of his wits.

"What's wrong with you?" said Froug. "You look like you've seen a ghost."

Croix turned back, but the Vagabond was gone.

"Where did you get that?" said Froug, noticing the sword.

"An old woman gave it to me," responded Croix, searching the crowd in vain.

Froug examined the blade. "Well, no wonder. It's dull as a rock. You won't be slaying anything with that."

Croix grabbed the sword and ran his wounded finger along the edge. His father was right; the blade was dull.

"It was sharp before," insisted Croix.

Froug wrapped his arm around Croix's shoulder. "Don't worry, I have a real treasure for you," he beamed, patting his pocket. "But not until tomorrow."

Croix smiled back, but his mind was elsewhere. He had already decided not to tell his father what the old woman had prophesied. He knew his father would just laugh and say she was crazy, and maybe she was. But he had a funny feeling about her that he couldn't shake.

Slowly, they made their way out of NorthCity. Croix looked back with regret, now knowing what he had missed growing up. A hundred yards ahead, the IMX transporters were lined up in their respective docking stations, waiting to return the Netpeople to their moons. He easily spotted the big, black UG IMX letters on the tail, short for "The Underground." As they walked closer, his stomach tightened. He was overcome with an incredible urge to run. He finally understood why his father had refused to talk about the wonders of the Net or discuss the other moons. It would have made life trapped in the Underground unbearable.

Croix looked up and whispered, "Do we have to go back?"

Froug took his hand. "It's just for three days, then we'll go home. But until then, I have to do my job."

Croix knew it wouldn't be long, but suddenly he couldn't bear to return. Up ahead, a final booth caught his eye. In it, a colorful old JavaMonk was holding court in front of a mesmerized group of Netpeople. The sign above the booth read, "Eleusis, Moon of Great Mysteries."

"Come on, Father, just one more," said Croix, running ahead.

"We'll miss our transporter," Froug called after him.

"It will just be a minute," Croix called back.

A young PageBoy, no more than ten years old, stood enraptured in the center of the booth, captivated by the JavaMonk's tale. Croix squeezed in beside him. The name "Red" was tattooed on the PageBoy's hand.

"There will be devastation across the land," the Monk foretold. "Disease will run rampant and we will be cut off, alone and desperate to survive. But in our darkest hour, when the Gates of Destruction open, He will come."

"Who?" shouted Red.

"They call him Netman," the Monk continued, "His ancestors came from a faraway land. He was sent here to save the Net and its people from complete destruction. He will walk among us until the demons that threaten our land are destroyed forever."

"When's he coming?" demanded Red.

The Monk continued, ignoring him, "Soon, he will come. He will appear first to a boy in the ElectronicForest, but not in a form recognizable as his own. Beware, for the time is coming!"

"Wow!" said Red, turning to Croix, who stood with his mouth ajar, amazed at what the Monk had said.

"We're going to miss the transporter," said Froug suddenly, yanking him away.

Croix walked away slowly, dragging his feet.

Froug noticed Croix looking back and nudged him forward.

"They're just a bunch of crazy old men," Froug said. "They'll tell you anything for a good trade." They boarded the crowded UG IMX, packed with sorry souls making the journey home. Croix caught a few staring enviously at the "C" branded on his hand. He tucked his hand into his pocket and turned away just as the doors closed, pinning him against the small window of the transport door. Croix noticed Red walking onto his transporter. He barely caught the name of Red's moon as the Underground transporter zoomed off. It read, "EF IMX"—the ElectronicForest.

Five

THE MELTDOWN

Later that night, a fierce solar storm kicked up, throwing eerie shadows on the wall of Croix's bedroom. The open window rattled with each gust of wind. Croix tossed and turned in bed. He finally sat up. Thunder boomed in the distance, but the cries of the VirusVultures circling the VirusPrison could still be heard.

Croix mustered his courage and ran to close the window. He hated these nights. As he pulled down the window, he noticed the heavy smoke coming from the stacks of the VirusPrison, looming ominously on the mountaintop in the distance. "I won't miss you," he muttered, slamming it shut. The thunder stopped momentarily, but the flashing light continued. Croix was relieved. He spotted his sword in the corner of the room and curiously walked over to it. He touched the sword's blade; it was sharp! In the flashing light he wondered if it could be a magic sword. He waved it in front of his long bedroom mirror, feeling its weight and power. He advanced, slicing the air with it. His jabs became fiercer as he danced about the room, pretending to fight a ferocious Virus who stalked him. Taking the Virus by surprise, Croix plunged his sword into its chest. The creature fell in a heap. Croix raised his sword in victory and proclaimed, "I am the Scorpion Prince."

At that moment, a thunderclap exploded, sending Croix running for cover. Pulling the covers up to his neck, he watched with fear as the familiar silhouette on the wall transformed itself into the Shadow Virus, Croix's childhood bedtime tormentor. With the covers pulled tight, he tried to tell himself he was just imagining it. After all, he was the Scorpion Prince; nothing could hurt him. But, as the image grew near, his fear grew stronger. He pulled the covers over his head and squeezed his eyes shut, praying, as he always did, that it would go away and leave him alone. The Shadow had haunted him for years, filling his head with negative voices. He desperately wished he could be brave, courageous and fearless, but sometimes, it felt hopeless.

Froug entered Croix's room dressed in his Prison guard uniform. He quietly hung a tattered cloth over the window to block the light. Croix peeked out from under the covers, relieved to see it was his father. "Don't cover it," said Croix.

"What are you doing awake?"

"It's the thunder," said Croix, sitting up.

"DeathPing is moving in," said Froug, referring to the storm. "Try to get some sleep."

As Froug tucked him in, Croix noticed the uniform. "Where are you going?" he asked, alarmed.

"They just radioed me. The Prison's shorthanded tonight, but don't worry, it's only until morning." He ruffled Croix's hair. "I'll be back before you wake up."

Croix caught Froug's hand. "Please don't go."

Froug sat down beside Croix. "I know things haven't been easy. It will get better. I promise." Froug pulled a ruby-red velvet pouch out of his pocket, adding, "I was going to wait until morning for this, but—" He handed Croix the pouch. Croix smiled, untying the string around the top. A flat, shiny emerald stone tumbled out. It hung on a leather cord.

"Wow," said Croix.

Froug tied it around Croix's neck. "It will protect you against all evil."

"Thank you," said Croix, fingering the round stone in awe. He hugged his father tight. "I'll never take it off."

"Now try to get some rest," said Froug, getting up and covering his son. He lovingly stroked his hair and whispered, "I'll see you in the morning." But Croix had already drifted off to sleep.

* * *

Froug ran up to the patrolling guards as a noxious smoke poured into the catacombs. "They need me down in DeepFreeze. Cover for me," he said, handing them his roll call list and hurrying down the hall.

"What about us?" called back a stricken guard, struggling to breathe.

"What's wrong with the generators?" called another. "We need help up here, too."

Froug acknowledged them with a wave. He was just following orders.

Asylum paced nervously in the security command center. He stood at the console of the expansive glass booth overlooking DeepFreeze below, wondering when it would all end. The giant computer panel that monitored and regulated DeepFreeze was ablaze with flashing red lights. Sirens repeatedly sounded on the floor as the temperature rose. He watched, anxiously, as two guards frantically tried to fix the circuitry problem. Losing patience, he shouted, "Get me Harper and Fiske!"

"But sir, we can't keep moving the guards to DeepFreeze," argued the senior guard. "The catacombs won't be secure. We could have a blood bath on our hands."

Asylum slammed his fist on the console. "If we don't secure this sector, we will have a blood bath! Lock down the Prison!"

The guards exchanged nervous glances. A lockdown was a last-ditch effort used to protect the Net in case of a complete Prison meltdown. They hoped Asylum was overreacting. They keyed the code into the console. Within seconds, the bridges around the Prison rose and the moat flooded with a bright green radioactive solution. When it mixed with the moat's scalding-hot springs, lethal gas vapors created a wall of poison no one could escape, including the guards. They were now locked in with the Viruses.

Froug entered DeepFreeze and found himself in five inches of water. "Oh, my God," he said under his breath. The casings were melting all around him. Guards ran frantically to repair Virus monitoring devices as alarms sounded everywhere. Froug sloshed through the water to a nearby guard who was hastily repairing a monitor. "What's happening?" he yelled over the noise.

"We can't get the temperature regulated," replied the guard. "The colder we make it, the warmer it gets. The systems are going haywire. We're trying to load into our backup generator and have the remote system manage the temperature settings, but it isn't responding."

Asylum spotted Froug on the floor and radioed down to him. "I need you in operations," boomed the voice through Froug's radio badge. "Get that evacuation duct open, now!"

"Yes, sir!" replied Froug, splashing across the cavernous room to the operations center that controlled the Prison systems. Froug knew they would all die if they couldn't get the evacuation duct open. Not only would it drain the water that would soon fill the DeepFreeze chamber, it also served as an escape tunnel that led into the streets of the

Underground. The duct had been built into the Prison as an afterthought, for use only in lockdown situations. It was their only way out.

Throughout the operations room, guards worked feverishly to repair the Prison control systems. Smoke streamed out of the main generator. Electric shorts flashed as the rising water burned out circuitry. Froug ran to the main duct. He knew that it hadn't been opened in years.

Froug found the emergency panel and popped it open. It was worse than he thought. The circuits were corroded and wouldn't respond to any commands. It would take hours to replace them. Froug called to the guards nearby. "Help me open the hatch."

"It's two tons of solid steel. We can't pry it open," argued one guard.

"We have no choice!" said Froug.

Five guards jammed steel bars under the lid in the floor.

"On the count of three," ordered Froug. "One. Two. Three!" They heaved with all their might, but it was useless. The circular hatch wouldn't budge. Froug could feel the water lapping at his shins. It had risen another two inches.

The ice was now melting at a rapid rate. The heads of the Viruses were thawing, their eyes starting to shift. The putrid odor of the creatures filled the room, making the men cough and gag as they tried to work. It was unbearable. Asylum radioed Froug in the evacuation chamber. "What's the status?"

Froug's transmission was filled with static. "We're still trying, sir. The circuits are burned out. We're trying to manually dislodge the hatch."

Suddenly, BeelzeButt's hands crashed through the ice and grasped the bars around the casing that held him. The bars began to bend under his incredible force. Asylum flipped on the central communication system and yelled, "Code Blue! Every man to DeepFreeze! NOW!" Alarm horns blasted through the catacombs. Puppet, MoonRat and HogHead watched gleefully as the guards scrambled down to DeepFreeze.

Asylum radioed to Froug, "Stay down there and get that bloody thing open!"

The guards raced into DeepFreeze and stopped dead in their tracks, paralyzed by the unbearable stench and horrifying sight of three hundred of the Net's most vile creatures waking from the dead. None of their training had prepared them for this.

Froug worked feverishly in the operations room, alone. Outside, the fierce magnetic storm raged on. He tried electrical surge rods, pluton lasers and small explosives, but nothing loosened the cap. He reached for a lever from a high shelf when, through a small window, he saw a brilliant explosion of red light illuminate the village below. He gazed out, wondering for the first time if he'd ever see Croix again. He shook the thought from his head and went back to work.

The guards waded down the aisles armed with fire blasters and got into position in front of the casings. Each was assigned six. Asylum gave the order over the communication system: "Don't fire your guns until the Viruses have completely thawed, otherwise you'll waste your fuel on the ice and flood the chamber with water," he warned. "Remember, you won't have time to reload."

Chunks of ice crashed to the ground around them as the Viruses came to life, their grunts and screams filling the air. Asylum radioed to Froug.

"What's the status?"

"It won't budge. I've tried everything," Froug radioed back.

"Use the D9 explosives. Blow it open."

"But sir, the explosion will cut through the catacombs and release the Prisoners," argued Froug. "It will compromise the Prison."

Asylum looked out, resigned, as the heads of every Virus twitched to life with ferocious energy. "In a few minutes, it won't matter."

Froug ran to the red high-security box marked "D9 explosives." He punched in his code and opened it. He quickly laid out the bomb mechanism and began to assemble the explosives on the hatch. He had seen this done only once, and struggled to remember the proper sequence.

Half-thawed, the Viruses savagely ripped back the bars with all their strength. The men watched in horror, fingering their triggers, anxiously, cautioning each other: "Not yet, not yet."

Suddenly, The HeadHunter Virus, a savage tribal beast, ripped open his bars and jumped. Panicked, the guards opened fire, melting the ice casing and flooding the chamber within minutes

The Viruses dropped throughout the room, splashing into the water and attacking the guards one by one. It turned into a blood bath as each man fought desperately for his life.

BeelzeButt carefully surveyed the scene below. He spotted his escape—the operations room. He immediately broke through his casing and jumped down. A guard, fighting off the BeastBomber—an apelike Virus with razor sharp teeth—turned just as BeelzeButt released his deadly spray. The guard covered his face, screaming with agony as the VirusSeed ate through his skin and traveled to his heart. He collapsed into the water, twitching, his face barely recognizable.

Froug loaded the last of the device on the hatch and uncoiled the wire that led to the detonator. He walked backward slowly, carefully draping the coil overhead, out of the water's reach. He tried to focus, but was shaken by the tortured screams that grew louder as he neared the door. He could see the Viruses mercilessly butchering the guards. Body parts were strewn about the room; the water was a sea of red.

Froug hurried. He knew there was no time. He stood by the exit of the operations room, about to push down the detonator handle when he felt a tap on his shoulder. He turned.

"Let me help you with that," said BeelzeButt, spraying Froug with his deadly venom.

Froug collapsed in a convulsing heap on the detonator, sending a massive explosion ripping through the chamber and upper floors. The secret tunnel lay exposed, water rushing down into its hole. BeelzeButt escaped into the passageway as hundreds of Viruses followed. The few guards that could still walk staggered to the tunnel as the Prison erupted in flames.

Asylum staggered in, struggling to right himself, blood oozing down his chest. He spotted Froug on the floor gasping for breath. "Hang in there," he whispered, lifting him up. "We'll get you some help."

A wasteland of bodies covered the muddy grounds at the foot of the evacuation duct exit near the village. Asylum stumbled out of the tunnel carrying Froug, who labored to breathe. He carefully laid Froug down on the grass, before collapsing dead.

***

Croix awoke to the sound of a giant explosion. He ran to the window and watched in horror as flames consumed VirusPrison. Grabbing his sword, he ran out in desperate search of his father. Emergency horns sounded everywhere. Croix ran behind the panicked townspeople to the tunnel exit. Pushing his way through the crowd, he strained to make out the faces in the sea of carnage ahead. Something caught his eye. He stopped, spotting his father among the tangled bodies.

"Father!" screamed Croix, running blindly through the men. Froug weakly opened his eyes and saw Croix just yards away. Mustering all his strength, he yelled, "No!" Croix stopped just feet from his body.

"You'll be infected. GO!"

A final blast rocked the mountaintop, sending Croix flying back with the force of the explosion. The villagers ran screaming at the sight of the Viruses pouring out of the tunnel and charging through the streets. Croix lay on the ground, stunned and motionless. He watched in horror as BeelzeButt approached and kicked his father over. Seeing Froug still breathing, he doused him again with another load of his deadly venom, killing him instantly.

Croix snapped. Consumed by rage, he got up and charged after him, no longer caring if he lived or died, desperate to avenge his father's death. BeelzeButt and the other Viruses quickly boarded a nearby transporter. As it was about to take off, Croix hurled himself at its door and dragged himself inside just as it closed behind him. The transporter flew off, leaving behind a deadly sea of Viruses hatching from the remnants of their victims' bodies.

Six

NETMAN RETURNS

DeathPing had finally passed. The morning was sunny and unusually quiet on HighBand. You could see for miles across its crystal-blue Cyberwaters and there wasn't a soul in sight. Suddenly, the shattering sound of a sonic engine broke the silence. It grew louder and louder until, out of nowhere, five rockets shot out of the water and flew two hundred feet into the air before crashing back down, creating a massive tidal wave. Surfing out of the hundred-foot barrel just as the gigantic wave closed out, crushing anything in its breach, exploded Netman and the CyberSquad!

    With his long, agile body glued to a fluorescent green RocketSurfboard, Netman blew through the curl powered by his sonic Backnose Propulsion

System, named for the sizable flared nostrils at the back of his tall, amphibianlike head. "You call that fast?" he yelled back to Didgit. "Watch this!" he challenged, racing off with his blond tuft of hair fanning back with the force of his speed.

Didgit cruised up directly behind him on her RocketBoard, her blond ponytail flying. "Is that as fast as you go?" she teased. He looked back smiling, clearly impressed. The two, similar in appearance, made a powerful team. He killed the Viruses, and she repaired the damage they wreaked on the Net. Behind them, Ramalamadingdong, a timid, stocky two-legged Cyberwarrior known as Ram, flew out on his outstretched enormous rainbow-colored horns, propelled by the same Backnose Propulsion System. "Hey, wait up!" he called. Unlike the others, Ram was afraid of Viruses and hated battling them, which, as the CyberSquad Virus expert, posed a bit of a problem.

Krash and Burn, known as the Kickstart twins, were the exact opposites of Ram. Young, wild kids, they fearlessly picked up the rear, pulling Rodeo 540s, snowboarding-type stunts, off the lip as they ripped down the wave on their Boards. "This beats the simulation room," yelled Krash. "Yeah! Can't wait to hit some snow," replied Burn. Hanging down from their colorful skullcaps were transparent eye shields that gave them supernatural telescopic vision and sensory perception.

Minutes later, the group pulled up on the far side of HighBand, and straddled their Boards. Suddenly, Didgit yelled, "Watch out!" They dove out of the way just as a metallic Orb hurled out of the sky and crashed into the water, barely missing them.

They remounted their Boards as the door to the Orb, known as a MessageLog, popped open. Out stumbled a seasick Messenger, a highly classified virtual Cybercourier from NetWatch exclusively able to travel between Thrae and the Net with relative ease—sometimes. The Messenger, a bit wet and disheveled, but relatively composed given his rocky landing, resembled a short, upright elephant stuffed in a formal bright blue tuxedo jacket, with regal Hindu-design tattoos all over his large floppy ears. "Sorry," he announced with a British accent, "I missed my bloody mark." The others laughed.

"My name is Mahotma," he said. "You can call me Hotma. I'll be your courier. I'm afraid to report, old chaps, that the whole lot of Viruses in VirusPrison have escaped and are threatening to destroy the Net. Lousy first assignment, frankly. Here are your orders," he said, handing Netman a glowing computer chip in a crystal vial. "NetWatch has provided you with all the information you will need for this mission." Netman carefully removed the chip and inserted it into a small compartment on the side of his XK3 Netwatch. "Your transporters, weapons, devices and anything else you could possibly need are waiting for you at your Hideout. That will be your base of operations here. Don't delay. We only have two days left before the Passage Gates open. Good luck." He disappeared into the Orb and vanished.

The CyberSquad members synchronized their titanium Netwatches to Netman's frequency and downloaded the mission orders. Netman hit the small red stem on the side of his watch and instantly the voice of Weldon Wall, anonymous, but somehow familiar to Netman, played over a map of the Net on the small screen. A flashing red light on the map illuminated K45, the Cray moon.

"Netman, you must go to Cray immediately and seek out Blocker," instructed Weldon. "She will have information on the Viruses' where-abouts and plans. She will also arrange for a guide and a transporter to take you to your Hideout. Everything you need to hunt down and recap-ture the Viruses will be there. The Meta-hackers are threatening to take over the Net in an attempt to gain control of Thrae. We must stop them and secure the Net in time for the opening of the Passage Gates, or the Chosen will be turned back forever. The attached file has the history and logistics you will need for this mission. We are counting on you." The pic-ture faded.

"Well, that sounds easy," said Ram sarcastically. Burn splashed him in the face.

"What?" asked Ram. "We don't know the first thing about this place." Netman hit the download button on his Netwatch and transferred the file into their respective Netwatches.

"We do now," responded Netman.

"Looks like RazorRapids will be the fastest LowBand entry point to Cray," said Netman, checking the tracking device on his XK3.

"Are you ready?" he asked the group.

They nodded.

"Remember," warned Netman, "don't fight the current when we get to the whirlpool. Just enjoy the ride."

"We got the file, boss. Thanks." countered Didgit.

Netman winked at her and said, "Well, let's go!"

They powered off in flank position with Netman at point, cutting deep paths down the expansive ocean, creating ten-foot wakes. As they approached the massive, churning whirlpool, they slowed down. Netman motioned for them to go no further.

"When I give the signal," Netman instructed, "plunge straight down the opening and don't stop until you fall into LowBand. Krash and Burn," he called, "no teasing the Piranii."

"Oh, come on!" squawked the twins.

"Piranii are nothing to joke about. They'll tear your head off in one bite," scolded Ram.

"Yeah. Yeah. Yeah," they scoffed.

Turning to Netman, Ram said, "You know there might be a few safer routes back the other—"

"Sorry, big guy. We don't have time."

"I'll cover you," offered Didgit, smiling. She couldn't help but be amused by Ram's blatant vulnerability. Whether she liked it or not, he was her responsibility. Without him, she knew she'd be unable to revive the Virus-ravaged Netsystems across the Net. Ram was their power source, the magic energy that infused life into dying systems. He was also capable of refueling their Backnose Propulsion Systems; thus they gladly tolerated his insecurities.

"Use your defenses only if necessary," warned Netman, "and whatever you do, don't slow down!"

Netman paddled to the opening, initially letting the suction of the whirlpool pull him down. Just as he was sucked in, he powered on his Backnose thrusters and gave the signal to the others as he dove into the whirlpool cavity with great force. Krash and Burn eagerly revved their Backnoses and dove in next. Didgit pulled up to Ram and advised gently, "Keep it powered all the way down and don't worry." He smiled nervously. He loved Didgit. Deep down he had a crush on her and desperately wanted to impress her, but his cowardliness constantly got in the way. He thought she was the coolest Cyberchick around. Who else could keep up with Netman?

The Piranii—giant, piranhalike Viruses—swarmed around the outside of the whirlpool in dense schools waiting for a meal. It had been months and they were ravenous. Every few seconds, a Piranus jaw, lined with needlelike teeth, punched through the force of the cone, snapping viciously in all directions before the suction of the whirlpool whipped it out. Netman raced through the prickly obstacle course using his board as a shield, dodging jaws with ease. Netman knew better than to lose his concentration or he'd be snatched up by their jaws and sucked through the whirlpool wall into their feeding territory.

Krash and Burn took a different approach. They descended rapidly, but tried to lure the Piranii by bodysurfing on their RocketBoards along the outer walls of the whirlpool. Using their advanced sensory perception, the twins could spot an imminent Piranus attack a mile away. As the Piranii broke through the cone, the twins took turns clocking them over the heads with their StunClubs, frying them dead out of the water.

Thanks to the brain mapping, Netman and the CyberSquad instantly inherited their NetWatch donor's quirky relationships. Didgit watched from above, resigned. She knew it was no use lecturing the twins on safety. They reminded her of Netman when he was little: fearless, brave and reckless.

Ram held tight to his RocketBoard, tucking in his big horns so they wouldn't get clipped. He squeezed his eyes shut, repeating the mantra: "Go straight. Go fast. Go straight. Go fast," as he dove straight down the middle of the whirlpool not daring to look.

Netman broke through the floor of the whirlpool first, landing in a small brook in LowBand that fed into the RazorRapids. The others crashed in one by one.

Didgit and Netman, using their Netwatches, morphed their boards into sleek RiverRacers, turbo water-blaster boats that could withstand and maneuver the rocky falls of the RazorRapids. Krash and Burn jumped in with Netman, while Ram hopped in with Didgit. Netman set out first, with Didgit following.

The RazorRapids ran through a lush, tropical valley filled with exotic birds and animals. The beautiful and tranquil terrain lulled travelers into a false sense of security as they descended the pristine waters. Farther ahead, however, the river turned murky, and became treacherous, its churning waters dotted with sharp rocks that jutted out unexpectedly at every turn. The sweet chirping birds and indigenous animals were replaced by stalking Viruses that had long ago infected the wildlife and transfigured them into deadly, life-sucking creatures.

"JunkModemPoles ahead," warned Ram.

Netman sped up the boat when he spotted the slithering school of JunkModemPoles swimming right for them. Heads of deformed and hideous creatures from ModemPole crashes topped the snakelike Poles. They were infected NetWaste known for their radioactive electrical currents that could kill on contact. Krash and Burn stood at the bow, ready for them. They unclipped the front latches of their boots, and prepared to release "the Goo." As the Poles neared, Krash and Burn shot streams of a sticky, fluorescent orange substance from the fronts of their boots into the water. The oncoming Viruses swam right into the Goo slick, getting trapped in the gummy mess. The more they fought, the further entwined they became. The twins high-fived each other, yelling "Gooed ya!"

Ram stared nervously at the littered shoreline. It was covered with remnants of transport vehicles and bones of Netpersonnel who didn't make it. It was clear how this "Valley of Death" had earned its name.

Just then two human-size vultures, known as CarcassRats, swooped down from their nests unnoticed, heading straight for the CyberSquad. Ram turned back just as one swooped down and grabbed Didgit with its claws. But before the CarcassRat could take flight, Ram blasted it with his FireHorns. A fiery red beam of light shot out from the tips of his horns, frying the creature. The vulture dropped like a rock, right on Krash. Crawling out from under the scorched, oozing Carcass, wiping rancid flesh from his face, Krash yelled, "What are you doing?!"

Ram scrunched his shoulders apologetically. "Sorry."

Krash pushed the Carcass into the water. "Shoot that-a-way," he said, pointing overboard.

Ram waved. "Got it."

Didgit and Netman shared a knowing look. It was going to be a long day. The waters settled down as they passed through two tall canyons, signaling they had made it through the Valley of Death. Here, the RazorRapids poured out into the expansive ModemPoleRiver, the entrance to Cray. Netman spotted a tall signpost floating ahead in the water. It read, "Entering RedMarb K45—Cray. Watch your step." As they passed the signpost, the boats suddenly plummeted down into an invisible water shaft that opened up out of the sea, engulfing them.

Seven

THE CYBERBOUNTYHUNTER

Ram's horns turned white as they plunged straight down. Then, as if controlled by an invisible source, they slowed as they reached the bottom, and gently straightened up as they exited the chute and entered an enclosed water port. Ram finally let go of his tight grip on the side rails of the boat and looked around in amazement as they floated into a massive nine-story hub built around a five-mile-long waterway. The place was crammed with various docking stations for transporters and private vessels. The upper floors bustled with millions of Packets dashing to make their connections for their final destinations.

Netman and Didgit vaporized their RiverRacers and sneaked unnoticed with the others into the hull of a nearby DataTransferBus, or DTB, as it was known. The Packets, small football-shaped creatures, marched onto the DTB. Some carried parts of electronic messages, others pieces of file documents, while the elite transported bits of financial data that, when assembled, created information at their destinations. Packets were considered NetFootSoldiers, traveling nonstop from one place on the Net to another to keep the information flowing.

Once checked through NetCustoms, Netman and the others breathed sighs of relief. They could hear the Packets talking upstairs. One said to another, "How about a cold Neer at the NetJetServiceStation Cafe?"

Netman and Didgit exchanged a look. That's where they were headed.

The second Packet responded, "Thanks, but I just got new orders. They're shipping me out to Sakar on a Backbone."

"Nice knowing you," said the first sarcastically. "I hear that's murder."

As they arrived at the base, the Packets quickly jumped off the DTB and assembled single file for inspection by the HeadRouter, who diligently reviewed their orders, ensuring they were headed to the right address using the fastest route. During the commotion, Netman and the others sneaked out and followed the Packet who was headed to the cafe.

The group quickly shape-shifted into JavaMonks to blend in. JavaMonks were spiritual leaders, although not especially respected. They traveled the countryside filling the minds of poor Netpeople with supposed nonsense about destiny. It was a Net rule that they were permitted Intermoon travel. However, given the recent danger, fewer and fewer were traveling.

Netman squinted in the bright sunlight, admiring the information-processing chaos going on all around. Cray was the Net's main transport hub. All information exchanged across the Net eventually went through Cray. The streets were filled with Repeaters, Gateways, Bridges, Watermarks and other NetTransportation Netpeople racing to and from the base. Squadrons of Packets raced with their battalions across the airstrip and onto waiting Intermoon Backbone Transporters or IBTs. Every two seconds, one zoomed off to a different destination.

They stopped when they saw the Packet enter a ramshackle bar at the end of the strip with a pulsating neon sign outside that read, "NetJetServiceStation Cafe."

"That's it," said Didgit.

"Wait here for me," said Netman, lifting the black hood of his long robe. "I won't be long."

The NetJetServiceStation Cafe was a glorified transporter stop. The old barn-wood floor was usually covered with sawdust from the chop mill out back used to cut up and recycle broken transporters. The bar was big and long with red stools that stood high against the counter. The nicest places to sit were the booths along the window, if you could find an empty one, and didn't mind the inch-deep dead NetFlies along the sill. The patrons were legendary for being real roughriders; some were just passing through while others worked at the base.

The owner was Blocker Malone, a small but tough woman who put up with no nonsense. The men liked her and knew not to try and push her around. And since it was the only place in town to get a decent meal, they knew to mind their manners. But one patron, Iso, always gave Blocker a hard time. She didn't mind; she gave it right back.

Iso, an out-of-work Cyberwarrior, was in his usual foul mood. He had a secret crush on Blocker and, although he played hardball with her, it was all an act. He just wanted to take her out, but nothing ever worked. She rebuffed him even when he didn't know he was being rebuffed. But it wasn't hard to understand why. Standing six-and-a-half-feet tall with a flat head, squat legs and an enormous mouth that made him look like a deformed giant, it was difficult to get people to love him, especially since his favorite way to get attention was to bully people. At the cafe, at least he wasn't alone—misery loved company.

"Hey Blocker," Iso called. She motioned for him to wait a minute as she rang up another customer. Blocker had been on edge all day with the news of the VirusPrison breakout. She hadn't been able to find out much except some rumors. There had been no confirmed Virus sightings by any of the men.

She walked over, her tight shirt and cropped pants clinging to her petite, boyish frame. Her big brown eyes and thick lashes made up for the strange oblong shape of her face and perky ears that jutted out on either side.

"Yeah, handsome, what can I get you?" she asked.

Iso pointed to a glass. "Give me another Neer. And this time, no foam."

She winked, ignoring the slight. The bell above the door rang as it opened. Blocker turned to see who it was.

Netman walked in and sat down at the bar, making sure to keep his eyes low so as to not draw attention. Blocker couldn't put her finger on it, but there was something about him that made her think he wasn't a Monk. She glanced at her Comm7 monitor under the counter and checked the secret code that she was to exchange with Netman to ensure it was him. The Comm7 read: "X349hytd." She erased it and brought a warm cup of Noffee over to the Monk. Noffee was a local specialty that warmed up the boys and kept them alert for their long flights home.

She placed the cup in front of him and asked casually, "What will it be?"

"I'm afraid I'm lost," Netman responded. "I'm looking for an address."

He pulled back his draping sleeve and showed her the display on his Netwatch. Seeing the code, she said smoothly, "Why, yes, let me show you our map." He followed her to the back of the bar, into a dusty little room. The IBTs could be heard overhead as they blasted straight up into HighBand. Iso couldn't help but notice their exchange. He watched suspiciously as they disappeared down the hall.

In the room, Netman lowered his hood and shape-shifted into himself. Blocker stood stunned at the transformation, unable to speak. She had heard about him for years through NetWatch, and his legend was well known on the Net, but she still couldn't believe he was standing before her.

"Blocker, where's my Neer?" called Iso from the bar.

She snapped out of it at the sound of Iso's voice. "In a minute," she yelled back.

"I don't have much time," said Netman. "Do you have any information about the Virus breakout?"

"Not much is known," said Blocker. "There was a meltdown at the Prison. The heat sensors went crazy and burned up the place. All the Viruses escaped, including everyone in DeepFreeze. The NetRuler has not told anyone officially. He doesn't want to cause a panic. But some of the NetLeaders have been to the Underground and have seen the devastation. The whole moon has been sealed off. No one is allowed in or out. The rumor is that the Viruses are heading for the desert plains of the Sakar moon, where BeelzeButt is calling a meeting of the VirusColony to plot the takeover of the Net." Netman suddenly felt outnumbered.

Iso leaned back in his stool and peered down the small hall, wondering what was taking Blocker so long. Tired of waiting, he shuffled off after her.

"I'll need a transporter and a guide to take me to the Hideout in the ElectronicForest," said Netman.

"Hey!" yelled Iso, approaching. "What do I have to do around here for a Neer?" Netman shape-shifted back into the Monk.

He walked in, adding, "If the Monk's lost, have him use his magic powers to find his way home," Netman looked down obediently. He knew no one liked the Monks. They were considered a strange breed.

"Actually," said Blocker to Iso, "you're going to help him."

"Help him!" exclaimed Iso. "Since when do I do charity work? I'm a CyberBountyHunter, not a nurse."

"Since you'll be paid your full fare for a half-day's journey and you owe me on a healthy three-month tab," said Blocker, "that's when."

Iso cringed. He didn't like to be talked to that way, but worse than having his ego hurt, he knew she was right. He had been out of work for a long time, and if it hadn't been for Blocker he wouldn't have had a warm meal in months.

She continued. "So, what do you say? One trip and we're square. The Monk's already paid me."

"Well, wait a minute," whined Iso. "I negotiate my own—"

"I think, given the circumstances," said Blocker, cutting him off, "this is more than generous."

Resigned, Iso asked Netman. "Where are you headed?"

"I'll direct you once we get to the ElectronicForest," responded Netman.

"All right," said Iso to Blocker. "But then we're even, right?"

Blocker smiled and gave him a wink. "Come see me when you get back." Iso blushed, not knowing why.

"There are a few others outside," said Netman.

"Oh, no," said Iso, shaking his head. "I agreed to take you, not a whole clan of you crazy Monks."

Blocker gave him a threatening look. "What does it matter? The IBT is plenty big." She shook her head, muttering under her breath, "Always such a grump."

Netman followed Iso out, stopping at the door. "Thank you," he said, turning back to Blocker. "Wish us luck."

"You won't need it," she said, smiling.

"That's what you think," mumbled Netman, exiting.

An hour later, Iso sat grumpily at the controls of the transporter as it rocketed out of the Portal. The transporters always left from the outskirts of each moon so they could ascend immediately to HighBand. Just above the clouds in HighBand the atmosphere turned pitch black. They had entered Cyberspace.

Netman and the others sat in the back, still disguised as Monks in their traditional black robes. However, Ram's shifting abilities were not working properly. He was in a robe, but little else had changed.

Iso turned to Netman and motioned towards Ram in the back, "Who's the freak with the horns?"

Netman leaned in, whispering, "We took him in a year ago. Poor guy, he never got proper treatment. The legendary BigMamboHorn Virus got him. Maybe you've heard of him?"

"Never," responded Iso.

Ram sat nervously, trying to nonchalantly stuff his big horns into his small hood.

"He's sensitive about the horn thing," continued Netman, "I wouldn't mention it."

"You're a weird group, you know that?" said Iso, turning back.

Sitting in the co-pilot seat, Didgit choked back a laugh. Dressed in the traditional blue robe of a female JavaMonk, she stared out the cockpit window keeping an eye out for Virus transporters. Female monks were rare, but known to possess special powers that were tied to the forces of the universe. "Are you from Cray?" she asked.

"No, I'm from Vajra," responded Iso. "I used to be a great warrior, worked for the Cyberforces fighting Viruses. Then I went off and became a CyberBountyHunter. Paid better."

"Is it true about the breakout?" Didgit prodded.

"Don't know anything about it," answered Iso curtly. "I make it my business not to know. I used to be the Consortium's hired gun. They couldn't do enough for me then, but after I got infected by NeonSniper, they dumped me. Years I worked for them, and what did it get me? A life banished to this place. Now I leave the fighting to the Cyberforces."

"Maybe someday there'll be a cure," said Didgit.

He laughed mockingly. "You got some special powers?"

She turned away, smiling at the quiet skies. "Could be."

Eight

THE VIRUS TRANSPORTER

Huddled in an oversize barrel in the Virus transporter's cargo bay, Croix bolted awake, wet with sweat from his nightmare.

He had dreamt he was alone in VirusPrison searching for his father. He wandered aimlessly in the burned-out, deserted catacombs, calling for him in the dead of night. Suddenly, a cell door slammed behind him. Whipping around, he saw his father inside a cell, tied up and gagged. Croix pulled desperately at the cell door but it was locked. Without warning, hundreds of Viruses oozed out of the cracks in the walls, attacking his defenseless father. Croix screamed and begged in vain for them to stop as they ravaged his body, but it was too late. Froug slumped over, dead.

Croix tried to shake the image from his head. But he kept seeing his father struggle helplessly as he looked on. The truth was, Croix couldn't forgive himself. He felt responsible for his father's death. He had watched BeelzeButt murder him. If it were the last thing he did, Croix would get BeelzeButt.

Small rays of light filtered through the woven Cybervines of the barrel, revealing the sea of two-inch, black metal balls that Croix sat in. He repositioned his sore butt and grimaced with pain. He didn't know how long he had been asleep, but he suspected it had been hours. He picked up two of the balls and nervously rolled them in his hand while he tried to focus on a plan. The enormity of what he had taken on began to settle in as he realized he was trapped on a Virus transporter with no way out.

Suddenly, the transporter dropped and lurched left, sending everything in the hull flying. Croix hung on as the transporter leveled out and the barrel righted itself. From behind, he heard a cage door swing open, followed by a ferocious growl. He slipped the balls quietly into his pocket and picked up his sword.

An oddly mutated creature stood in front of his toppled cage, relieved to be free. The name on the cage read "P.A.Y.O.R.," short for "Pet At Your Own Risk." He was a Crog, half crocodile and half dog. Sitting on his short hind crocodile legs, he stood three feet tall. The Crog scratched his belly and looked around hungrily, his long floppy ears perking up as he caught a scent. He zigzagged across the cargo deck, his long, pointy snout pressed to the floor, sniffing wildly until he stopped at the barrel. The Crog licked his chops and ripped into it with his razor-sharp teeth. The strong Cybervines began to give way. Croix sat paralyzed, not knowing what to do.

The hull door abruptly flew open. LipVirus, one of BeelzeButt's lieutenants, waddled in carrying a box. Standing less than four feet tall, Lip was a fat, grotesque walking head. His beady eyes sat far apart on opposite sides of his huge Venus-Flytraplike face, the lower part of which was all lip, with pointy fangs drooling over it. His squat arms and legs seemed stuck on as an afterthought.

Payor froze, but Lip spotted him immediately.

"You stupid Crog!" yelled Lip, advancing. "Those are explosives!" Payor cowered, whimpering.

Lip grabbed Payor and threw him down a trap door in the floor marked "Head Refuse." As he flew down the dark pit and splashed to the bottom, Lip yelled after him, "You wouldn't have it so good if you weren't BeelzeButt's Crog."

Croix heard Payor's thrashing and desperate whining before Lip slammed the lid shut. For a moment, Croix actually felt sorry for the creature, but was relieved it was gone. Lip carefully picked up another box and carried it to the exit. Croix peeked out of the hole just in time to see Lip punch his code, "LV359," into the wall panel. The hatch slid open and Lip walked out.

Croix knew it was now or never. He lifted the lid off the barrel and peeked out. The coast was clear. He could hear the Crog splashing below, struggling to stay afloat. Croix recited the number over and over in his head as he hurried to the hatch, his sword in hand. He punched in LV359. The hatch slid open. As he was about to exit, he heard the Crog howl out desperately in the pit. Croix could only imagine what was down there. He didn't know if it would help, but he ran back and popped the lid. Payor was shocked to see Croix's face peering down the hole at him and even more surprised when he left the lid open. For a moment, Payor relaxed and stopped thrashing. It was then that he noticed the small handles in the long steel tank. Payor managed to catch the first handle and pull himself up high enough to grab the next. Slowly, he eased himself out of the pit and eagerly looked around for the boy. But Croix was gone.

Nine

ELECTRONICFOREST

Deep in the ElectronicForest, Red toiled away on the inside of a twenty-foot-high WebPage. His cap read: PageBoy 22545. He was repairing a malfunction on the screen of a snowboarding Website. The image of the snowboarder kept exploding as he careened down the slopes. He suspected it was the work of CrabViruses. The sign hanging on the WebPage read, "Under Construction." The PageBoss, an older, stockier version of #22545, sporting a white beard and a healthy paunch, walked in.

"What's taking so long?" he screamed as he caught sight of the sign. "The clients are threatening to pull the site!"

Red hurried down the long ladder with his heavy PageToolbelt clanging against his hip. "It's riddled with CrabViruses, Boss. I've tried everything, but I can't get rid of them."

"Well, you're not leaving until it's fixed! I don't care if you're here all night!" The PageBoss stormed out. Red kicked the ladder. He hated his job; it was a dead end. Everyone in the ElectronicForest did the same thing. Everyone was simply a clone of each other. Red wanted to be different. He wanted...adventure.

Outside, a horn blew. Thousands of PageBoys, identical except for their different-numbered caps, walked out of their Pages and marched single file down WebPageRow, a Cybercountry road lined on either side with infinite billboardlike WebPages. Red watched them, shaking his head. It was another monotonous day like all the rest.

Red grabbed his satchel and dragged out the red electronic book, entitled *Netman*, that he had purchased on the black market in NorthCity. He flipped through to the secret compartment in the back. Inside the false back of the book, he pulled out the hidden map to Netman's Hideout that had cost him six months' savings. But it was worth it. He knew Netman held the key to changing his future, or so he hoped. Scrawled at the top of the map were the words, "The Secret Trail to Netman's Hideout." Red had heard about the catacombs below the ElectronicForest that led to the Hideout, but he had never known how to get there...until now.

* * *

On the transporter, Iso pointed to the small GreenMarb Moon a thousand miles away. "There it is," he said.

Everyone got up from the back to get a good look. They couldn't help but feel excited to see it at long last—the ElectronicForest. Iso knew there were several ways into the ElectronicForest, but he favored his secret entry. Few knew of it, and those who did rarely took it.

Netman watched silently as Iso began his descent, wondering which way he would go. He had to be careful because Monks knew little about transporters and space travel. "Are we taking the BlueLake Route?" Netman asked innocently.

The BlueLake trajectory was notorious for its dangerous GippoViruses who hid around its waters, but it was considered the safest LowBand entry point to the ElectronicForest. The only drawback was that it left you in a remote section of the Forest.

"No, I have my own way," responded Iso grumpily.

They descended to twenty thousand feet above HighBand. A tropical forest appeared in the distance. Netman grew concerned. He was afraid Iso was taking the LavaTube Route, which was the fastest and most direct entry point, but also the most dangerous. It was typically considered foolish to take such a big risk merely to gain fast entry. Netman knew there were hotdog pilots who loved the thrill of racing the LavaTube, but not many lived to brag about it.

Ram cleared his throat and asked nervously, "Where are we going, Iso?" Netman flashed Ram a warning look.

"I'm taking the LavaTube," Iso responded. "Don't worry, we'll be in and out in a minute."

"Do you think that's safe?" Didgit pressed.

"Look," he snapped, "You paid me to fly, now let me fly this thing!" He pulled up the controls, mumbling, "Backseat Monks!"

Netman signaled for them to take their mission stations. He knew this was going to be a bumpy ride.

As they drew nearer, the group could see a towering, smoking volcano rise up out of the center of the island, its lava bubbling and exploding into the air. Ram shook his head. He knew this was trouble. He had strong intuitive powers, and although the others teased him about his "feelings," he was rarely wrong. He knew only Netman had the speed and agility to outmaneuver the Lava. Ram thought Iso was either one hell of a pilot or one stupid Netguy. He hoped it was the former.

Krash and Burn pressed their heads against the small flight deck windows, not wanting to miss a minute of the dive.

"Buckle up," Iso called back.

Moving up to the front, Netman asked, "Do you mind if I sit here and watch?"

Iso shrugged. "Suit yourself, but keep it quiet."

Netman nodded in agreement. He knew that the key was a combination of timing, speed and quick maneuvering. It was critical to get into the mouth of the volcano precisely as the Lava receded and exposed the LavaTube that ran along the core of the volcano, finally exiting in the heart of the ElectronicForest. But if they got lost in the maze of LavaTubes at the bottom, within seconds the Lava would be on their backs, burning everything in its path.

Didgit counted the seconds between recession and resurgence of the Lava. She confirmed they had only twenty-eight seconds to get out before the Lava came pouring in after them. As the Lava receded, she set her watch to countdown. Iso gave it full-throttle. Ram closed his eyes and hung on. The LavaTube opened up before them. Iso dived into the mouth of the volcano and flew straight down into the fifty-foot wide tunnel. They zoomed at top throttle speeds. Twenty seconds left and counting.

Netman was impressed with Iso's skill. He knew it took a lot of guts to maneuver a transporter like that. But he also knew this was the easy part. It was a straight shot. Ram opened one eye, but quickly closed it when he saw that the wings of the transporter were within inches of the tunnel walls. One false move and they'd crash. Didgit glanced at her watch. Eight seconds remaining.

They were running out of time. At the end of the long tunnel, they hit the infamous fork. Of the three possible ways before them, only one led out. Netman knew Iso had to take the tunnel on the left. But even if he did, they still would have to maneuver through the shortcut's deadly maze. Suddenly, they heard the Lava explode and felt the walls shake. Didgit's Netwatch beeped. In seven seconds, the Lava would be on them.

Iso slowed at the forked intersection and took the left turn. Netman breathed a small sigh of relief, but knew it would still take a quick right, a second left, and finally a third right to escape safely. Didgit could see the Lava heading down the trail. She looked at her watch. They had three seconds left.

Iso jogged right and accelerated before he turned left. It was a tight turn. He had to nearly stop to not crash. Netman looked back quickly. The Lava was gaining on them. But before Netman turned back, Iso jogged left instead of right. "No!" screamed Netman, but it was too late.

The blood drained from Iso's face when he saw it was a dead end. Iso immediately cut the main engines and reversed the thrusters, screeching the transporter to a stop just inches from the rocks. Lava barreled down the tunnel straight at them. Netman yelled, "Get on the rocks!" They flew out of the escape hatch and scrambled up the rocks. In the commotion, Iso didn't notice Netman and the others had shape-shifted back to themselves. Netman yelled, "NOW!" All five pointed their CyberRayGuns at the wall above. Their red beams blew a hole through the dense rock wall. "Run!" yelled Netman. They flew through the opening just as the Lava overran the transporter, exploding the craft and propelling them to the lush forest below.

Dazed from the crash, Iso stood up slowly, shocked to see Netman and the others were no longer monks. "Who are you?" he demanded, pointing his LaserGun at Netman

"I can explain," said Netman.

Just then, a screaming MonkeyDropperVirus swooped down from a tree, knocking Iso off his feet and sending his gun flying. The monkey's deafening screech sent hundreds of monkeys flying out of the trees, charging Netman and the others. Iso struggled as a monkey tried to sink its fangs into his neck. Netman and the CyberSquad fired their CyberRayGuns, but the MonkeyViruses kept coming.

"K4!" yelled Didgit. The others ducked and held their noses as Didgit shot a payload of K4 gas from her Backnose onto the monkeys, making them spin and convulse before they turned and attacked each other.

Catching sight of an unaffected monkey about to sink its venomous fangs into Iso's neck, Netman fired his DeathRays. A deadly beam of Nitrovapors shot from his eyes, shattering the MonkeyVirus into a million pieces, leaving only a clear ViceCube with its frozen VirusSeed in the center. The other monkeys ran.

Netman strolled over and picked up the cube, tossing it to Krash.

"Put that on ice, will you?" Krash popped a latch on his boot revealing a freezer compartment and dropped it in.

"How did you do that?" asked Iso, getting up.

"Oh, just something I picked up. I hate to do this to you, but I have no choice," said Netman, stunning Iso with his CyberRayGun. Netman caught him as he slumped over.

"Why didn't you kill him?" Ram demanded.

"He's coming with us."

"With us! We can't trust him. We don't even know him."

"Like it or not, he's all we've got," said Netman. "By the looks of it, we're going to need all the help we can get. Besides, he's a good pilot and a brave warrior. We can never have too many of those."

"But he knows too much," argued Ram, "and it's dangerous to let anyone know the whereabouts of our Hideout. If the Viruses find out, they'll discover our entire arsenal. We'll be defenseless."

Netman handed Iso's slumped body to Ram. "Exactly. So, you take him and make sure he doesn't wake up on the way."

"Fine," said Ram, struggling with Iso's weight, "but I have a bad feeling about this. Someday this will come back to haunt us."

Krash and Burn rolled their eyes at Ram's incessant ramblings about doom and gloom. Ram flew off, barely able to hold Iso in his short hoofs. Netman, Didgit, Krash and Burn flipped on their watches and materialized their NetLugeRacers, long, wide skateboards with retractable wheels for hovering or Cyberstreet racing.

"Guys ready for some fun?" asked Netman.

"Yeah!" yelled Krash and Burn, jumping on. Hovering inches off the ground, they took off like rockets and zoomed through the trees.

"Wait for me," protested Ram from above. "There are Viruses out there."

Ten

THE ENCOUNTER

Red walked along for hours, but he wasn't sure which way the map went anymore. He turned it sideways, upside down and right side up, but it still didn't make sense. The markings were impossible to follow. Red checked his watch. He'd have to head back soon. It would be getting dark and he was starved. He pulled a Netcompass out of his pack and headed for the clearing ahead to stretch out and take one last look at the map.

Cutting through the last bit of forest, he heard a twig snap behind him. He turned around. Nothing. He stepped up his pace. Maybe this Netman thing was a stupid idea, he thought. The map was probably a phony. He looked back again, but there was nothing there. He relaxed as he turned around—and walked right into the ChickenChoker!

"Looking for me?" The ChickenChoker asked.

Red took one look at the giant viral beast and did an about face, screaming at the top of his lungs as he ran, "HEEEELLLLLPPPP!" He ran as fast as he could, but the ChickenChoker was closing in, his ten-foot-long arms nearly swiping Red off his feet.

***

Ram rocketed down through the trees, meeting the others who waited by the quicksand pit, the secret entrance to the Hideout. Ram was clearly out of breath as he lowered Iso down. "Somebody else take him, please!"

"Don't worry, old man," said Krash. "We've got him." Krash grabbed Iso's legs, while Burn took his arms. They carted him off into the quicksand pit, which parted as they entered it, revealing the hidden stairs to the catacombs below.

Just then, they heard a scream and saw Red running through the dense trees headed right for them. The pit closed.

"Shape-shift," ordered Netman.

The three changed back to Monks just as Red ran out of the forest screaming, "HELLLP M—"

The Choker choked off his last word with his viselike grip.

"I wouldn't do that if I were you," said Netman, suddenly appearing in his Monk's garb.

The ChickenChoker snatched the Monk by the neck with another hand and said threateningly, "And you are?"

Netman shape-shifted right between the Virus' fingers and responded, "Netman!"

The Chicken Choker's eyes bulged out and he bolted, screaming at the top of his lungs.

Netman lifted up Red, whose mouth was still agape from witnessing the shape-shifting.

"Are you *the* Netman?" asked Red.

"The one and only."

"Wow!" said Red, amazed he had actually found him.

"What are you doing out here?" asked Netman.

"I was looking for your secret Hideout and got lost. See," said Red, proudly handing him the map that he was still clutching.

Netman examined the crumpled map. "I'm afraid they robbed you," he said.

"Oh," said Red, disappointed. "Figures. I spent my savings on that dumb map."

"You better get home now," said Netman.

"Hey, Netman?" asked Red, turning back. "Is there any chance I could get your autograph? The PageBoys all make fun of me. No one else believes you exist."

Netman looked back at Didgit and Ram, still in their Monks' attire. They nodded, but motioned for him to hurry it up.

"Sure, why not," said Netman, flattered. He burned his name into the map using his DeathRays and handed it back.

"Wow!" said Red, staring at the signature.

"Take the path to the right, it's a safe route. And tell those PageBoys to have some faith."

"You bet."

Red headed off, pleased with himself. He turned back to wave good-bye, but Netman and the others were gone.

* * *

An hour later, Iso slowly regained consciousness in the Hideout's medic room. While he was unconscious, Didgit had performed viral heart surgery and removed his VirusSeed. It sat in a small canister on her shelf, wriggling away in a bloody mess.

"What happened?" asked Iso, coming to.

Didgit gently lifted his head and pressed a small, clear cup filled with a bright orange liquid to his lips, "Here, drink this," she said. He sipped slowly. "You'll feel better soon."

"Where am I?" asked Iso.

"This is our Hideout. Its location is secret, so we had to knock you out."

He sat up slowly, getting his bearings. He noticed the red VirusSeed larvae in a clear test tube on a nearby tray. A chill ran up his spine. "What's that for? " he asked suspiciously.

"It's for storage now. I removed them from you."

"From me? But you can't do that. No one can survive that procedure."

"You can here," said Didgit. "We have special energy fields that suspend the body, allowing it to tolerate the surgery. I don't know if I got all of it, but it will buy you some time. Judging by the size of them, you didn't have much left."

Iso ran his hand over his chest, and for the first time in years didn't feel the slithering of the Virus larvae inside that made his skin crawl. "They say you get used to it, but the truth is you never do."

"Would you like to dispose of them?" she asked.

"Sure."

"Follow me."

Iso followed her down a long spiral staircase that led to a basement. A metal door slid open as she approached. They descended a few steps into a thirty-foot-long freezer. It was a mini DeepFreeze, filled with twenty VirusSeeds all floating in small, frozen ice casings hanging from the ceiling.

She pointed to one. "Set it in there."

Iso dropped the tube into a casing while Didgit hooked it to its cable stabilizer below. Immediately a purple liquid poured into the casing, freezing the Viruses dead in their tracks. The larvae seemed to shrink and age.

"It's not going anywhere now," said Didgit. "My mission is to discover an anti-Virus serum to ward off infection and to discover how to safely destroy the seeds without risking further contamination. Unfortunately, all we can do now is contain them."

Iso followed her back up to the medic room. "What did you give me? I've never felt better."

"Netade. It heals and rejuvenates the body, making you stronger and more powerful than ever before."

"How can I ever thank you?" asked Iso.

"You can help us," said Didgit.

"Who are you?"

"Come. You'll see."

Iso followed Didgit up to the main floor and climbed up the stairs to a catwalk and into a CyberVator. The moving chamber rose through a cavity to the seventh floor. The doors opened, revealing a cavernous transport hub. Iso stepped out, but stopped at the sight of the sleek, hundred-foot-long silver transporter rising up before them. It had the same Backnose Propulsion System used by Netman and the CyberSquad. Painted in black letters on its tail was "NetShuttle." He followed Didgit inside.

Netman and the others sat at the main console on the flight deck, checking the systems. Netman smiled when he saw Didgit and Iso. "Are you feeling better?"

"Yes, thanks," responded Iso. "You have quite a doc here."

"She's the best," said Netman.

"Yeah, yeah," said Didgit, embarrassed.

"I guess you're wondering what this is all about."

"You could say that," said Iso.

"We're running out of time, so I'll get right to the point," said Netman. "We're Anti-Viruses, the only ones of our kind. My name is Netman. And this is the CyberSquad: Didgit, Ram, Krash and Burn." Each member nodded respectively. "You're not *the* Netman?" asked Iso.

"Yes."

"The legend?"

"Yes."

"But I thought that was a fairy tale."

"What is it with you Netpeople?" asked Netman, teasingly. "Doesn't anyone believe?"

"Who knew?" said Iso defensively.

"Our ancestors began their work on Earth's Internet, but not with much success," explained Netman. "An earlier version of myself was launched on the Net many years ago, but crashed after a short period of time. I'm hoping the same won't happen again."

"Wow!" exclaimed Iso.

"We need your help. Our mission is to stop BeelzeButt and his VirusColony from taking over the Net. They're planning on striking in force when the Passage Gates open," said Netman. "We must stop them or the Netpeople are doomed."

"But how?" asked Iso.

"BeelzeButt is headed to Sakar to assemble the VirusColony and plot their strategy. We must infiltrate the meeting and find out their plan. We could use your help; you're a good pilot and warrior. You're free to go if you choose. We can erase your memory. Or, you can join us and fight the VirusColony to restore peace to the Net."

Iso rubbed his chest. "I've been wanting to kick some Virusbutt for a long time," he said. "When do we leave?"

Netman smiled. "Now. Get up here, and I'll show you how to fly this thing."

Krash quickly closed the hatch as Burn programmed the computer to open the Hideout's rapid-exit portal above. A large eye-shaped opening in the ceiling of the hub slid open for takeoff. Burn gave Netman the thumbs-up.

"Buckle up," ordered Netman.

They hung on as Netman rocketed straight out of the hub and disappeared through HighBand toward the outer reaches of Quadrant D, en route to the deadliest moon on the Net, Sakar.

Eleven

SAKAR

The next day, the sands blew hard on Sakar's desolate desert plains. The sun storms, which had temporarily subsided, were back. The wind had picked up, sending hundreds of small, two-headed DartLizards scurrying for cover. RodentViruses, hairy desert rats found only on Sakar, burrowed deep into the sand, leaving only their black beady eyes peering out, ready to pounce on the first unsuspecting Lizard. It was the Rodents' favorite weather. As the Lizards darted over the sand, the Rodents snapped up and yanked them under, dragging them down to their dens, where they could savor their tasty meals.

It was common knowledge that all infected Netpeople, if left untreated for more than a few minutes, eventually spawned deadly clones of the Viruses that infected them, stalking the Net and doing their masters' dirty work by infecting others. Even with treatment, life expectancy was rarely more than a few years. It was rumored that eventually the infected withered away to nothing but small viral insects and rodents who clawed their way through the desolate moons of the Net desperately searching for food, a meal which typically meant eating what was once their own kind. It was a cruel food chain.

BeelzeButt stood by, watching as the men unloaded his transporter. He grinned, looking up at the VirusColony, a 298-foot-high, pyramid-shaped CybeeHive rising from the sands of Sakar. One of the wonders of the Net, it was in remarkable condition, surrounded on three sides by enormous sand dunes that shielded it from the storms. It had been forty-four years since BeelzeButt had been home. His ancestors had discovered the CybeeHive years ago and founded the VirusColony by laying claim to the entire Golden NG4 Moon, now named Sakar. Few dared to travel to Sakar, capital of all Virus activity. The Virus strains were well hidden under the sand, in the dunes and in invisible cocoons scattered throughout the desert. They lay in wait for unsuspecting Packets, BigEndians and other members of the Information Fleet that they could rob and infect. But mostly they used Sakar as a resting place to refuel, strategize and for some, replenish themselves with the moon's powerful Suckumen plant.

In the distance, BeelzeButt could see the last few transporters approaching for landing. It wouldn't be long now, he thought, before all the Viruses would be assembled and he could set his plan in motion. The Net would never be the same.

He yelled to his men, "Move it. We don't have all day!"

The compound around the Colony was buzzing with activity as various Virus strains unloaded confiscated food, arms and weapons from their stolen transporters. They had all been on a wild looting spree, pillaging every town and village along the way to Sakar.

Ten GadFlyViruses struggled against the wind as they staggered into the compound. They were working in twos, each one carrying the end of a long pole from which hung wheels of Suckumen, an unusual thorny desert plant. It was rumored that Suckumen gave Viruses special powers of strength when boiled down and distilled into a bitter alcohol. In order to get to the fruit of the plant, they had to climb up its tall, purple stalk and risk being nicked by its long, red poisonous thorns. If nicked, they died instantly. Only the most powerful Viruses had the able staff to collect the Suckumen. And only they consumed it. It was the drink of VirusLords.

Lip, along with Implant, a human-like Virus with four arms and various body parts sticking out of his Frankenstein-like head, struggled to carry a long, cannonlike weapon called the XRS200 through the transporter door. Croix hung on as he was bounced around inside the laser blaster. Thinking it was a relic, Croix had climbed inside to hide when he heard the Viruses coming. To his dismay, they carried it out, with him in it.

Croix reached for his sword and shimmied deep down into the barrel of the XRS so he wouldn't be seen. He desperately hoped the old Vagabond was right, that his was a special sword and that he was a warrior prince. He hadn't forgotten his father's gift, the magic stone that hung from his neck. He touched the cool stone, remembering his father's words, praying hard he was right.

BeelzeButt spotted them and yelled, "What are you doing? That's not a toy! Close that lid before you get us all killed!"

"Yes, BZ," they droned, struggling to put down the weapon.

Under his breath, Lip muttered, "Sure, ButtBrain, anything you say, Mr. BigButt."

Implant struggled with the weight as he put it down. "Whatever the ButtMan wants, the Big ButtMan gets, right?"

They rolled their eyes in unison. "Who made him the BigButt, anyway?" asked Lip.

"I think the Big ButtHole from Quadrant A in 1000BV," answered

Implant, wiping his brow.

"Figures, never trust an old ButtHole," remarked Lip, unhinging the big metal cap from the top and slamming it closed.

It went pitch black inside. Croix panicked. He could hear them locking him in. He desperately searched the cylinder for an air hole. His heart pounded with fear. Scrambling around, he discovered a small, partially obscured opening about two inches wide just behind him. He pressed his nose to it, breathing in the dusty air. He tried to breathe slowly and calm down, but he knew this was it. He was running out of time.

* * *

Netman, Iso and the CyberSquad raced up the side of a three-hundred-foot long sand dune on their turbo SandRunners. At the top, they dismounted and vaporized their vehicles. Lying on the edge of the dune looking down, Netman surveyed the activity below with his Bionetculars, virtual goggles that allowed him to scan the inside of any structure and "virtually" travel through it, creating a mental blueprint of the building.

Netman watched BeelzeButt disappear behind the Great Door into the Colony, followed by Implant and Lip pushing the XRS. The activity had died down as the final Virus transporter arrived with the last of their supplies. Suddenly, the Great Door closed. The compound was deserted.

Krash interrupted the silence. "I detect underground vibrations. Something is moving under the sand."

"It's a giant body mass, maybe one-hundred-feet long," added Burn, scanning the earth with his eyeshield.

"It's got to be the Great Wormagon," reported Ram. "He's the guard dog of the Colony."

"That can mean only one thing," said Netman.

"We go back to the ship?" asked Ram hopefully.

"No. They're starting the meeting," said Netman. "We have to hurry."

"We'd better move," ordered Didgit, looking off in the opposite direction.

"Thanks, Didg. I just said that," teased Netman.

"NOW!" yelled Didgit, pointing. They turned back to see an enormous swarm of giant, angry African Vbees headed right for them. Diving over the dune, they watched as the Vbees roared overhead and flew into the cone-shaped opening at the top of the CybeeHive.

"That's it!" said Netman, getting up.

"What?" asked Didgit, shaking the sand out of her hair.

"That's how we get in ... through the Hive."

"You know," said Ram, rubbing his stomach, "I'm not feeling so well. I'd better go back to the ship and lay down."

"And miss the fun?" said Iso, slapping Ram on the back.

Ram sadly shook his head, feigning disappointment. "It's a bummer."

"Nice try, Ram," said Netman. "I want you positioned on the southern dune. When I give the signal, fly to the top of the Hive and torch the entrance with your FireHorns. I want to see those Vbees pouring out of there in a fury."

"Oh, good," said Ram.

"Krash and Burn," continued Netman, "cover Ram as he tries to out run the Vbees. They're fast and they'll be shooting him with everything they've got."

"Cool," said Krash and Burn, looking mischievously at Ram.

"I feel better already," quipped Ram.

"Iso, you stay here and back up Krash and Burn. When Didgit and I are safely inside, I want you take the others back to the ship and get it ready to blast off as soon as we return. If BeelzeButt leaves before we get back, follow him. Don't wait for us. We'll find you. BeelzeButt has to be stopped at all costs. We have sixteen hours left before the Passage Gates open."

Netman and Didgit made their way down the dune carefully, so the buzzing Vbee guards, patrolling the entrance of the CybeeHive above, wouldn't spot them. The wind picked up, creating a violent sandstorm that obscured them as they darted across the compound to the VirusColony. At that moment, the ground beneath them began to shake and roll. It felt like an earthquake.

"Hurry! Climb the wall!" yelled Netman.

Didgit lost her balance and fell as Netman, unaware, scrambled up the ridges of the CybeeHive wall. Suddenly, the Great Wormagon broke through the sand and caught Didgit's foot in its large, oozing black claws, pulling her down below.

"Netman!" she yelled, barely audible through the gusty wind.

Netman turned and quickly fired his CyberRayGun at the Wormagon. It fell back stunned, releasing Didgit's foot. Didgit raced up the face of the Hive and joined Netman in a shallow cave in the wall.

The Wormagon burst up again, jamming its claws deep into their hiding place. This time, they simultaneously blasted him with their CyberRayGuns. The Wormagon collapsed to the ground, sending shock waves through the compound. They carefully climbed up to the top of the CybeeHive.

As soon as the guards moved out of sight, Netman signaled to Ram across the way using his DeathRays.

"That's it!" yelled Krash and Burn excitedly. Ram took off, flying straight for the cone-shaped entrance with his FireHorns fully extended. Hovering above it, he pointed his long powerful horns into the opening and fired directly into the Hive, burning and melting the whole inside core within seconds. The entire Hive immediately came charging out, releasing alarm pheromones. "Oh, no!" said Ram at the sight of them. He dashed back to the ship as the swarm of Vbees chased after him.

Krash and Burn fired at the Vbees with their CyberRayGuns as they gained on Ram, but there were too many.

"We better get out of here," yelled Krash.

"Run!" yelled Burn, darting for the Shuttle. They raced down, barely making it on board the camouflaged Shuttle at the base of the dune before Ram came screaming over the ridge and nose-dived straight into its open hatch, crashing to the floor. Iso slammed the door shut as the Vbees crashed into it. He started the engines, quickly putting up the defense shields as the Vbees continued to charge the ship. Ram got up, stunned from the fall, and straightened his mangled horns. He looked up, surprised, as the others began to clap. He turned beet red.

"Ah, it was nothing," said Ram shyly.

Iso slapped him on the back and said, "Good job. I told you it'd be fun! Now, let's take these critters for a ride." The shuttle took off, thousands of Vbees chasing after it.

* * *

Netman and Didgit entered the Hive's charred golden chamber. The combs were destroyed on the upper levels. Nothing remained except a molten honey-wax goo dripping from the ceiling and covering the floor.

"We better hurry, the Vbees will be back soon. But be careful, the walls are lined with deadly fungicides," warned Netman. "We need to get down to the bottom. These cells up here stored the honey and the level below stored the pollen, but below that are the Brood cells. That's where the VWorkers and the VDrones live.

"If we can get past them," he continued, "just below that layer are the peanut-shaped cells that house the VQueen's infants. Let's hope the VQueenbee is out." Didgit and Netman morphed on a protective outer coating and started the messy descent through the sticky core.

The place was eerily quiet except for an occasional dying buzz. They climbed down the spongy cells until they hit the Brood cells. There, several VDrones, with their bulging eyes, lay dead from Ram's fiery blast. They stepped over the bodies, moving toward a small hole in the floor that led to the den of the VQueen below. They slipped down and jumped out into the VQueen's private level. They were relieved to see it was deserted. Didgit pointed to an orange oval comb in the wall. "There it is," she whispered. "The entrance to her den."

They quietly climbed up into the comb and crawled along its soggy membrane, listening for signs of the VQueen. They cautiously entered her lair, a small, circular chamber, where the VQueen laid her eggs. There was no sign of her. Netman and Didgit looked around, mesmerized by the glistening golden beauty of the walls and sweet aroma of her honey. Twenty-five peanut-shaped eggs lay peacefully in a large round nest at the far corner of the room.

"Under the nest is the trapdoor that leads to the VirusColony. All we need to do is move the eggs and we're in," said Netman. "You watch the door. I'll get the eggs."

"I don't think so," objected Didgit.

"Why?" asked Netman.

"Given that she rips off the VDrones' testicles after mating, you can only imagine what she would do to you if she caught you with her eggs. It's a male thing."

"Right. I'll watch the door."

"Good idea." Didgit carefully removed the eggs one at a time. She looked admiringly at the sleeping VQueen infant in her arms, with its curled baby eyelashes and furry yellow-and-black striped head. She carefully laid down the transparent cocoon.

"You know, they're kinda cute."

"Maybe you'd like to baby-sit sometime."

"Very funny."

"Quiet," whispered Netman, peering into the comb.

"What's wrong?" whispered Didgit.

"I thought I heard something. It's nothing, I guess."

"Look what I found," said Didgit, moving the last few eggs out of the way. "A trapdoor." She wiped it clear and tugged on the handle. "It's stuck."

"Move over, Didg," said Netman, sauntering over.

"Here we go," said Didgit, annoyed.

"Let me show you," said Netman, throwing one of the eggs aside.

Suddenly, the VQueen charged in. "My baby!" she screamed. Before Netman knew what hit him, she doused him with her venomous poison, temporarily paralyzing him. The VQueen grabbed him in her claws, preparing to dismember him.

"NO!" screamed Didgit, throwing one of the eggs at her. The VQueen dropped Netman to catch her precious infant.

Didgit grabbed Netman and flung open the door, jumping down through and barely managing to slam it shut before the VQueen was able to charge through.

Twelve

THE VIRUSCOLONY

From his private quarters inside the VirusColony, BeelzeButt walked out onto his balcony, thirty feet above the ViralChamber, and surveyed the Virus activity below. The Viruses milled about the majestic hall whispering and carrying on. Some had taken their seats at the conference tables that wrapped around the large, multi-tiered room, facing the central dais, the "Floor" as they called it. However, most waited for BeelzeButt to first take his regal seat, presiding over the Floor with his first lieutenant, Leprosy B2, known as Leper.

BeelzeButt knew most were scheming to betray him. He didn't mind. In fact, he had counted on it. They had been incarcerated for a long time, and he knew they were dying to avenge themselves by wreaking havoc on the Net. BeelzeButt knew the key to controlling them was the XRS200.

Leper, a one-eyed protoplasm ball covered with oozing lesions, dragged himself in on his cane. A floating white tray, holding two small, glistening purple goblets decorated with precious stones and delicate gold BZ insignias, followed him. BeelzeButt stepped back inside to greet him.

"Is everything ready?" asked BeelzeButt.

"We're ready," answered Leper. He motioned to the tray and offered BeelzeButt a goblet.

"Good," replied BeelzeButt, satisfied. He lifted his glass and declared, "To complete dominance and rule!"

The Leper raised his glass and repeated the Virus mantra. "To complete dominance and rule!"

They downed the Suckumen tonic in one gulp and shattered the glasses in their hands, breaking out into maniacal laughter.

Not only did Suckumen give Viruses strength, energy and endurance, it also sharpened their senses and gave them heightened feelings of power and invincibility. For some, it had become an addiction. Over-consumption was dangerous and could short circuit internal viral systems, but since availability was scarce, it was a problem few concerned themselves with.

BeelzeButt stepped out onto the platform that perched off his balcony and waved his hand over the control panel. Immediately, the platform disengaged and floated down to the center of the Floor as the Viruses looked on in awe. Standing nearly seven feet tall, with scaly multi-toned, combat-green skin and an enormous, bulbous cranium that secreted deadly, vile venom, BeelzeButt was the self-appointed General of the VirusColony. He was their boss, but they hated him. If it weren't for his superior powers, they would have overthrown him long ago.

The platform floated gently to the ground. BeelzeButt stepped off and took his seat, calling the meeting to order. The Chamber seats were full of Virus representatives of every powerful and lethal strain. Only the "VirusBoss" of each strain was allowed entrance into the VirusColony.

Each one represented potentially hundreds of Viruses in its "family." The distrust and jealousy among the VirusBosses themselves was commonly known but not openly discussed. Although they publicly treated each with respect, privately they plotted each other's demise.

Still groggy from the VQueen's venom, Netman, along with Digit, slipped into the ViralChamber through a back door, as the meeting was about to start. The VirusColony servants, tattered JunkCreatures dressed in Netrags and old computer parts, drifted through the room carrying trays of Suckumen tonic for all to enjoy. Digit and Netman each quickly shape-shifted into one of them, picking up full trays from the serving table. Digit carefully laced the glasses with BluHare, a vile oil that slowly arrested the Viruses' internal systems, ultimately paralyzing them. Mingling through the Chamber, they offered any and all a glass of their special spiked Suckumen as they made their way down to the Floor.

Puppet, seated in front, eagerly snatched two and chugged them down. They couldn't get close enough to BeelzeButt, however. He was too well guarded.

BeelzeButt interrupted the raucous crowd. "Your attention, please."

The Hall quieted down. Netman and Digit listened attentively from the shadows of the room.

"Welcome to the VirusColony," began BeelzeButt. "For most of us, it has been a long road back. As you know, in just fourteen hours the Passage Gates will open, marking the eleven-year anniversary of the rotation of the sun. At midnight, the Chosen will line up to ascend to Thrae, while a new crop of Thraesians will be shipped down to be inaugurated as Netpeople.

"The hours leading up to this transfer are notoriously turbulent ones, with sun storms at their peak. It is a perfect opportunity for us to strike and take over the Net once and for all. Call it: Operation Crash. Thrae will be helpless without interplanetary communication, and the Thraesians will have no control over the systems that run their Planet. We will control their weather, their food, their water, their medical facilities and their defense system. The Consortium will have no choice but to surrender to us. They will pay greatly to use our Net, and the Netpeople will forever be our slaves. This will be the new republic!" The Viruses cheered wildly.

"But what about Netman?" interrupted a shaken ChickenChoker, downing another tonic. "I saw him. He was in the ElectronicForest. I recognized him from the last Cyberwar."

"Cut him off," ordered BeelzeButt, mocking him. "He's clearly had too much to drink." The other Viruses laughed.

"I'm telling you, I saw him," said Choker, turning to the others.

"I'm telling *you*," boomed BeelzeButt. "There is no Netman! What existed of that feeble Anti-Virus, I destroyed in 2078. You wouldn't be calling me a liar?" asked BeelzeButt threateningly.

"No," said Choker, shaking his head. "No sir."

"I didn't think so." BeelzeButt looked around with growing annoyance and disdain. "I thought you were ruthless, not some whiny, pathetic little variants! But maybe Prison got to you. Maybe you aren't what you once were. Maybe you don't have faith in the code!" A rumble ran through the chamber. The Viruses stomped and roared back, "Crash! Crash! Crash!"

"That's better," said BeelzeButt, motioning to Leper. The Viruses quieted down as Leper dimmed the lights and projected a three-dimensional holographic Netmap beside him. BeelzeButt pointed to the four quadrants that divided the Net and said, "Now, in exactly one hour we will split up and simultaneously attack the different quadrants of the Net. The FileInfector Viruses will take Quadrant A, and infect e-mail, WebPages, Websites and Newsgroups. The BootInfectors will take Quadrant B and infect all home-intelligence systems and transportation links. The MacroViruses will take Quadrant C and infect all files, databases and security systems. The Multipartite Viruses will take Quadrant D and infect defense and natural resource systems such as water, energy and food crops. I will take the Matrix.

"At exactly midnight we will convene there, and I'll lead the attack on the Servers, the Net's core. Together we will shut down what remains of the Net and bring Thrae to its knees!" The hall erupted in cheers.

"Now, HogHead will pass out the codes for your specific assignments." The snorting, piglike creature—a BeelzeButt lieutenant—walked up and down the aisles handing out the vials of code.

"You will see in your instructions that I have given each of you a moon of your own, which, in success, will be yours to rule as you see fit, without threat or interference from anyone in the VirusColony. In failure, you will get nothing."

BeelzeButt raised his glass and with his bellowing voice declared, "To complete dominance and rule!" The VirusColony shouted back, "To complete dominance and rule!" They downed their glasses of Suckumen, their faces first contorting at its bitter taste, and then quickly relaxing as they felt the tonic's invigorating effects.

"Why should we unite?" challenged a defiant Gargoyle, a notorious Virus. "Why not go out on our own and conquer whatever territories we want? We tried uniting once before and what did it get us? We all ended up in DeepFreeze." The Viruses grumbled in agreement.

"Because this time," said BeelzeButt, "We have a secret weapon!" He motioned to Lip and Implant. They wheeled the shrouded laser out to the floor. BeelzeButt pronounced, "Viruses, may I present to you the XRS200." He whipped off the cover, revealing the long, black single-barrel laser blaster. "The galaxy's ultimate laser blaster, capable of hovering, spinning and firing—all through mental telepathy. It can short out entire moons with one shot. When activated, the XRS is a walking time bomb, literally. It can propel itself across the Net and do our dirty work for us. In time, we will have a fleet of them monitoring the moons and ensuring obedience. It's the next-generation fighting machine." The room broke out in applause. "Come, see for yourself."

BeelzeButt threw open the lid. The air came surging in. Croix, nearly unconscious from lack of oxygen and desperate to escape, threw himself out, falling face first on the floor to the shock and surprise of everyone.

"Well, well, well," said BeelzeButt, prodding Croix with his boot.

"What have we here? A stowaway? And armed at that." Croix flinched as BeelzeButt's scaly hand reached down to grab his sword. BeelzeButt examined the dull blade and tossed it back at him, laughing. "That's some mighty sword!" The room broke out in guffaws.

Croix grabbed the sword, anger pulsing through his veins, and stood up, pointing his sharp sword at BeelzeButt. "You killed my father!"

BeelzeButt calmly looked down at the small boy and swatted the sword out of his hand. It slid across the Floor. "Did I?" asked BeelzeButt, stepping closer. "I'm so sorry." He suddenly yanked Croix up by the neck, dangling him off the ground. "I've killed a lot of fathers," he said, choking him. "You'll have to be more specific."

Croix struggled to pull the Virus' hand off his neck, but BeelzeButt was too strong. BeelzeButt noticed the "C" branded on Croix's hand and immediately threw him on the ground. Croix lay gasping for breath.

"Take him to my quarters," ordered BeelzeButt to Lip and Implant. "I'll deal with him later. Maybe then you can explain to me, *my security chiefs,* how a stowaway managed to board our high-security ship." Lip and Implant bowed obediently and dragged the boy away as the other Viruses snickered at their incompetence. BeelzeButt checked inside the XRS and, noting no one else inside, said, "Coast is clear, come on down."

Didgit and Netman emerged from the shadows still in disguise, having witnessed the whole exchange. They slipped out of the Chamber as BeelzeButt proudly showed the Viruses the XRS.

Running down the hall, Netman and Didgit shape-shifted back to themselves so they could use their powers.

"Who's the boy?" asked Didgit.

"An Underground runaway would be my guess. We'd better get him out of here before BeelzeButt gets his hands on him."

Netman, using his X-ray vision, scanned the rooms behind the doors but found nothing. The place was an endless maze. "We'd better split up," said Netman. "We'll never find him this way. Netman checked his watch. "If you haven't found him in ten minutes, go back to the ship. We don't have much time."

* * *

Lip and Implant dragged Croix into BeelzeButt's quarters. "I could take him," Lip ranted. "That pompous Butt. Where does he get off talking to us like that? He never talks to the others like that."

"He hates the others," Implant pointed out.

"Well, why doesn't he hate me?" whined Lip.

Implant spotted Payor in the corner, asleep in his cage. "Just throw him in there," he said, pointing to the cage. Lip kicked open the cage and yelled, "Get out! You worthless beast!" Payor rolled his eyes. He knew better than to snap at Lip. Payor got out and perked up immediately when he saw Croix.

Implant dragged Croix over. "Get in there," he ordered. Croix crawled into the cage, frightened they'd send Payor in after him. Implant slammed the cage door closed and locked it while Lip tossed Croix's sword into BeelzeButt's arsenal case and closed the lid.

Walking out with Implant, Lip warned, "Behave, Payor. BeelzeButt wants him alive."

No sooner had Lip and Implant walked out than Payor unlocked the cage door and stood excitedly waiting for Croix to come out. Croix didn't move. He thought for sure that Payor was going to rip him to pieces. Payor dropped to the floor and rolled over on his back. Croix was dumbfounded. He didn't know what to make of it. Getting no response, Payor ran to get his ball and threw it into the cage. "You want to play?" asked Croix incredulously. Payor panted happily, eagerly awaiting his toss. Payor obviously hadn't had a friend in a long time.

Not knowing what to do, Croix threw the ball in the air. Payor snagged it in mid-flight and tossed it back. Croix caught it laughing, amazed that this ferocious-looking creature was probably just harmless and lonely.

Croix threw the ball again. While Payor ran after it, Croix slowly crawled out of the cage. Payor ran back, happily dropping the ball at his feet. Picking it up, Croix asked, "Ready?" Payor barked enthusiastically. Croix slowly walked backward toward the arsenal chest, "You sure?" he said, stalling. Payor wagged his tail. Croix reached for the lid, yelled, "OK, go get it!" and threw the ball far across the room. As Payor ran after it, Croix grabbed his sword and bolted out the door.

Payor turned, hearing the door slam shut. His perky ears dropped when he realized Croix was gone. He lay down on the floor, letting the ball roll out of his mouth, and plopped his head on his paw. His first friend, the only creature who had ever showed him any kindness, was gone.

Croix knew if he weren't careful, he'd be discovered. He walked quietly down the hall, when suddenly, he heard BeelzeButt's voice and ducked into the first open room. It was a meeting room of sorts, with a long conference table, electronic boards along the wall and strange electronic devices on the arms of the chairs. He dove under the table as they walked in.

Puppet, Implant, HogHead, MoonRat, LockJaw and Lip—BeelzeButt's lieutenants—marched in, taking their assigned seats around the table. BeelzeButt, the last to enter, slammed the door shut. Croix crawled among the stinking feet to a safe spot in the center, desperately hoping none of them would accidentally stretch out and kick him.

"Now, look, I'm going to say this only once!" warned BeelzeButt. "And I do not want to hear any dissent. I divided up the territories amongst all the strains and that's it. We each got a region that we will patrol and own. We will abide by each other's boundaries and not attack. You will follow the plan, like it or not. Is that clear?"

They reluctantly nodded.

BeelzeButt continued, "I am not going to make the same mistake I made the last time. We have to stick together—at least until we take over the Net."

Puppet, a suspicious Virus with little loyalty, demanded, "But why give away Quadrant C?"

LockJaw, a tall, arrogant blockhead Virus, chimed in, "I did think that was rather generous."

The others grumbled in agreement. BeelzeButt slammed his fist on the table and shouted, "Enough! I am the General of the VirusColony and I rule! Anyone who doesn't like it can be eliminated." He leaned menacingly across the table. "Got it?"

Implant and the others bowed their head obediently and repeated, "Yes, BZ."

"Good."

The six had been arguing all day hoping to persuade him to cut out the other Viruses so that they alone could rule the Net. But BeelzeButt had been adamant.

"Besides, it doesn't matter now," added BeelzeButt. He flicked a switch, transposing a map of Thrae over the Net and smiled wickedly. "They'll each get a piece of the Net, but we'll get all of Thrae." The group looked up, shocked.

"How?" asked MoonRat, a vile, conniving Virus. "We've never been able to infiltrate Thrae."

"Yes, but we've never hitched a ride on a 'Chosen' one. You may recall children's frail bodies get to skip the brutal Virus irradiation treatment before ascending." The seven broke out in maniacal laughter at his brilliant plot.

Under the table, Croix began to shake uncontrollably realizing they were talking about him. He had to get out of there fast; otherwise, he could be the host responsible for destroying the Net and bringing the Virus plague into Thrae.

Thirteen

PAYOR GOES HOME

Minutes later, BeelzeButt stormed into his quarters followed by Leper. "What do you mean he's gone?" shouted BeelzeButt, searching the room.

"Lip said they put him in the cage," said Leper, pointing to Payor's empty crate.

BeelzeButt charged after Payor who sat huddled in the corner. "If you touched him, you're dead!" He pried open Payor's jaws and stuffed his head inside looking for evidence of foul play. Payor was horrified.

"Nothing!" exclaimed BeelzeButt, slamming his jaws shut. BeelzeButt turned to Leper. "I want this whole place searched. I want that kid, alive. And you, you stupid WatchCrog!" he yelled to Payor, "I'll take care of you later!"

The alarm sounded throughout the Colony. Outside, a fleet of Virus transporters revved up their engines, preparing to start Operation Crash. Croix ran blindly down a hall, frightened out of his mind and completely lost. He turned a corner and ran smack into LockJaw and HogHead. "There you are," said LockJaw, grabbing him. "You are getting to be quite a nuisance, aren't you?" Croix struggled to get free.

Pulling out his stun gun, HogHead added, "We'll take care of that."

Suddenly, Netman bolted around a corner and immediately fired his DeathRays, shattering the Viruses to pieces. He ran to Croix, "Are you OK?" he asked.

Croix nodded.

"Don't worry, I won't hurt you," reassured Netman. "I'm here to help. Come on, we have to hurry before they seal us in."

Croix looked up at him, remembering what the JavaMonk had predicted, and asked hopefully, "Are you Him?"

Netman paused for a moment, ruffling Croix's hair. "I guess I am."

Croix smiled. "Finally!"

In his quarters, BeelzeButt pulled his guns, lasers and magic sabers off the wall of his security vault, and packed them carefully into a large case. He stopped suddenly, hearing his door creak open. Grabbing a small saber from the wall, he stepped behind the door of the vault. Didgit quietly moved through the room looking for signs of the boy. Spotting the open vault door, she headed for the back. No sooner had she stepped in than BeelzeButt plunged the saber into her back, releasing its paralyzing venom. She collapsed.

Leper stormed into the quarters. "Sir, someone has infiltrated the Colony and taken the boy. LockJaw and HogHead have been iced." BeelzeButt walked out carrying Didgit.

"Who is that?" asked Leper, alarmed.

"Judging by her Backnose, I'd say she's with Netman. We have to keep this quiet. I don't want the VirusColony to know he's here or they may decide to foolishly strike out on their own. I'll be sure to finish him this time."

BeelzeButt handed Didgit to Leper. "Load her last and seal her in the tomb in the transporter. She'll make good bait. I'll get the kid and Netman."

Outside, the remaining transporters took off. Krash watched from the Shuttle. "They're leaving!"

"Did you see BeelzeButt?" asked Iso.

"No. His transporter is still on the ground," answered Krash.

"Figures. He's always last to go," said Iso.

Ram scanned the desert around the compound. "I don't see Didgit or Netman. We can't leave without them."

"We can, and we will if we have to," said Iso firmly.

Krash, Burn, and Ram silently shared a look, knowing better.

"You heard him yourself," Iso said defensively.

***

Netman and Croix ran through the complex until they made their way down to the lower sector. Netman knew exactly how to get out from here. They dropped through a secret hole in the floor, landing just below the compound. Netman scanned the maze of tunnels before them. They headed down the main tunnel when, out of nowhere, the ground began to shake and the Wormagon barreled down the tunnel, headed right for them. Netman jumped out of the way, pulling Croix behind him, but Croix lost his grip and fell. The Wormagon snatched up Croix in its claws, stuffing him into its slimy mouth. Netman jumped into its jaws, prying them open long enough for Croix to jump out. Struggling to keep the jaws from slamming shut around him, Netman yelled to Croix, "Stab it in its underbelly!" Croix stood, hesitating. "Stab it!" shouted Netman. Croix took his sword from his sheath around his waist, and closing his eyes, plunged the sword with all his might into the worm's underbelly. An explosion of brown mucous spurted all over his face. The worm reared up, releasing Netman.

He dropped to the ground, grabbed Croix, and sprinted down the tunnel as it began to collapse around them from the convulsing worm.

***

Krash surveyed the remaining activity in the compound. Suddenly, he spotted BeelzeButt and Leper exiting the Colony carrying an unconscious Didgit. "They have Didgit!" he screamed.

Iso grabbed the Bionetculars from him. He watched as BeelzeButt and Leper carried her onto the transporter and disappeared inside. "She's still alive or they wouldn't have taken her."

"They've started the engines," reported Ram. "What do we do?"

"Follow our orders, and go after them," said Iso.

"But what about Netman?"

"He can take care of himself," said Iso. "Prepare for launch." While Krash and Burn followed orders, Ram quickly sneaked down below into the engine room.

Dragging Payor's cage behind him, Lip boarded BeelzeButt's transporter calling excitedly, "BeelzeButt, the servants forgot Payor."

"You idiot!" yelled BeelzeButt, grabbing the cage. "I left him there on purpose!" He tossed the cage out into the desert. "I hope he dies a slow, painful death." Payor bounced around in the cage as it rolled to a stop in the middle of the deserted compound. The transporter door slammed shut.

Payor watched despondently as the transporter zoomed off, disappearing into Cyberspace. Suddenly, the wind picked up. RodentViruses, one by one, popped out from their underground holes. Payor watched uneasily as they scurried over and surrounded him, anticipating a tasty meal.

Netman abruptly shot out of a ground hole a hundred yards away, pulling Croix out behind him. "We better hurry and get to the Shuttle," said Netman.

Payor whipped around, hearing the voices. Seeing Croix, he barked ecstatically.

Croix turned. "Payor," he called, running to him. The Rodents dove for cover. Croix knelt down and opened his cage. "What are you doing here?" Payor charged out, licking him all over his face. "OK, OK, you're welcome," said Croix between licks.

"Is he your friend? asked Netman, approaching.

Croix looked down at Payor. "I guess so."

Netman smiled. "Very well, bring him along." Payor barked happily, jumping up and licking Croix. He followed them wagging his tail, elated he had a real master now.

Iso watched with growing frustration as BeelzeButt disappeared into Cyberspace. "What's the problem?" he yelled to Ram below. "We're losing him!" Iso hit the surge release button again. Nothing. It wouldn't power up.

Below deck, Ram snickered mischievously as he pulled the starter cap out of his pocket. Ram yelled back, "It looks like the engine's clogged from the Vbee stinger attack. It could take awhile."

Netman, Croix and Payor boarded the Shuttle unnoticed while Iso, Krash and Burn argued over the malfunctioning systems. "Hello?" called Netman.

They whipped around and hollered, "Netman!"

"What are you guys waiting for?" asked Netman. "We're losing him."

Ram came barreling up the stairs all smiles. "All systems go!"

Fourteen

THE MESSAGELOG TRANSMISSION

"What do you mean, *captured?!*" demanded Netman.

"We saw BeelzeButt and one of his men drag Didgit onto their transporter," said Iso. "She appeared unconscious. Before we could do anything, they took off."

Netman paced the floor. "I should have known better than to have sent her off alone. BeelzeButt wants something or he would have killed her."

"He wants me," chimed in Croix.

"You?" asked Netman.

"Yes," said Croix miserably. "He thinks I can get him into Thrae," said Croix, showing him the branded C on his hand.

"Iso, power up," said Netman.

"Where to?"

"The Matrix," answered Netman. "ButtBrain doesn't know what he's in for." Iso blasted off into the blackness of Cyberspace.

An hour later, Netman escorted Croix below deck. "I can't believe you survived all that."

"I'm lucky you came along when you did," said Croix.

Payor happily trailed them, although he wasn't thrilled to hear they were chasing BeelzeButt. Netman scanned his hand over the hatch sensor. It slid open, revealing compact but comfortable quarters with a pair of overhead bunk beds, a small galley, a crew desk and chair, and small wardrobe compartment.

"You can bunk in here," said Netman. "Ram will bring you something to eat and some warm clothes. You'll need them once we get to the Matrix. Get some rest."

Netman turned to leave, but Croix stopped him. "Thank you for everything. I feel like this is all my fault."

"BeelzeButt got us here, not you," reassured Netman. "We'll get Didgit back and we'll get you home, don't worry."

"I don't even know where home is," answered Croix, wistfully.

Netman pulled up a chair next to him. "My mother and father were killed by Viruses," confided Netman. "I was nine years old. I struggle to keep what few memories I have of them. Didgit, Ram, Krash, Burn and I are all orphans. You aren't alone. We created our own family, and you will too. I have to hand it to you, it took guts to get on BeelzeButt's transporter."

"It was stupid. But I couldn't just stand by and watch him walk away. I had to do something."

"It took a lot of courage to do what you did."

Croix cheered up. "You know, the old Vagabond at the bazaar in the NorthCity told me I would meet you. She called you, 'Him.' She said I was the Scorpion Prince and gave me this." Croix showed him his glistening sword with its razor-sharp edge.

"It's funny," said Croix, examining the sword closely, "sometimes the blade is sharp and sometimes it's dull."

Netman curiously picked up the sword and examined it. "Do you know where she got this?" he asked.

"It was on display, for trade, at the Vajra booth. I accidentally cut my finger on it when I was admiring the swords."

Netman flipped over the sword, stunned to see the Royal Scorpion Insignia on the handle.

Pointing to the Insignia, Netman said, "This means that this sword belonged to the legendary descendants of Anatares. The Scorpion sword was used to battle the Parasites and Viral Mutants of the Trapezium Galaxy before there even was a Net. It has magical powers, able to kill Viruses on contact. The legend is that only the people of Anatares have control over the Scorpion sword, otherwise its power lies dormant. It makes warriors out of boys and heroes out of men. Does the sword become sharp when you handle it?"

"Yes, but as soon as I put it down or give it to someone else, it turns dull."

"This was passed on to you for a reason," said Netman. "It's no accident that you were able to survive 'uninfected' in the Underground, and it's not a coincidence that we've met." Netman got up to leave. "I'll teach you how to use your saber. When we get to the Matrix, you may need it. You may have been born here, but your spirit comes from another land. Your time has come."

Croix sat astonished. He couldn't believe it.

***

Netman, Iso, Krash and Burn sat around the long chart table planning strategy, when Ram entered the high-tech war room.

"How is he?" asked Netman.

"Asleep. He dozed off after dinner," said Ram, grabbing a seat.

"Good. He'll need his rest."

"What's the story with the boy?" asked Iso.

"He is of Anatares decent."

"Cool!" exclaimed Krash and Burn.

"But they've been extinct for hundreds of years, wiped out by the Parasites in the Disaster of 909 BV," argued Ram.

"Apparently, the spirit of one survived, and he's below deck," answered Netman. "He told me his mother was infected when she bore him, but mysteriously he was born disease-free. Stupidly, the Consortium never made the connection. A small number of the Anatares people were selected for anti-parasite serum testing. He might be the sole genetic survivor of that work."

"Then he's immune to infection?" said Ram.

"Could be," said Netman. "Luckily, BeelzeButt didn't know that. But he isn't immune to destruction."

"Croix could hold the key to Didgit's work on developing an anti-Virus serum," said Ram excitely.

"It's feasible," said Netman, walking to the Netmap. "But first, we have to stop them from destroying the Net. We're running out of time. The Viruses are fanning out across the Net as we speak. When they convene at the Matrix at midnight tonight to bring down the Servers, we'll strike. If we can hold them there, we have a shot at saving the Net. If not, it's all over."

The room grew quiet. "How do we do it?" asked Iso.

"Simple. We go fishing."

"Yes!" shouted Krash and Burn, high-fiving each other.

"Oh, no!" said Ram vehemently, shaking his head. "It's too risky. You can't set a trap and capture four hundred Viruses with just five of us."

"With Didgit and Croix, we'll be seven," corrected Netman.

"OK, seven of us?"

"We'll beat them by exploiting their greatest weakness," said Netman.
\nd what's that?" asked Iso.

` distrust and jealousy among them. We will divide and conquer...
'ast resort, if he's willing, we'll use Croix as bait."

Hours later, Croix sparred in the glass encased virtual-battle gym. He stood in the center of a dimly lit room and fought holographic images of Viruses in the jungles, oceans and mountains of the Net. Croix started to relax and get the hang of it as Netman coached him from outside the booth.

"If you hesitate, you're dead. Once you commit, always attack."

Croix plunged his sword into the belly of the Mammoth Virus. He grinned as he successfully pulled his bloody sword from the defeated beast. Netman kept them coming at Croix as he danced around the floor, dodging lasers, sabers and physical attacks from the Viruses. Netman smiled as Croix loosened up and began to have fun.

"Never stay still," instructed Netman. "Keep moving. You have to be able to react at a moment's notice. Don't show any fear. They can smell it."

Burn entered the room. "Netman, they need you upstairs. A MessageLog transmission is coming in."

"Burn," called Netman, "Take over."

Burn slipped on Netman's ZX1 Netshades in time to see Croix getting strangled by the BeastBomber Virus. "No! No!" yelled Burn, exasperated. "You should have seen him coming a mile away. Now, once more, and this time, tap into your extra-sensory perception and try to feel their energy coming at you." Burn started the attack again.

Netman entered the bridge as the weak audio and flickering video transmission came through on the screen. Ram fiddled frantically with the console switches.

Hotma appeared on the screen. He reported gloomily in his British accent, "Netman, the Viruses are on a rampage. The moons are being destroyed as we speak. The ElectronicForest has been completely ravaged by infection."

Croix and Burn bounded up the stairs to join the group.

"Things are even worse on Cray," continued Hotma, "See for yourself." He transmitted real-time footage from the scene. Blocker frantically ran around treating the sick that were arriving by the DTB-load at the

NetJetServiceStation Cafe, now a makeshift medical center. BigEndians and Packets staggered in; some on stretchers, with leeches stuck to their faces and serpent worms slithering on their bodies. They had obviously been infected en route, carrying information to their destination.

"Except for the wounded being flown in for treatment, Cray is at a standstill," reported Hotma. "All Packets have been grounded, and the uninfected are being quarantined. It's pandemonium everywhere. People are boarding up their shops and homes, afraid of what might be lurking out there."

Iso watched, broken-hearted, as Blocker ran around with the aid of only a few others, tending to the sick. She was overwhelmed and in real danger of contracting the infection herself. "Get out of there," he muttered under his breath.

Hotma switched to exterior shots of Thrae. "The Virus attack on the Net is wreaking havoc on Thrae as well. We have no power," he continued, "no method of communication. The water supply has been contaminated and the food supply is dwindling."

They watched in shock at the pictures of the deserted streets, covered with rubble from collapsed buildings.

"The Viruses have taken over the Net's weather and the seismic controls of Thrae. Earthquakes are destroying the planet's infrastructure. It is a struggle of man against machine as malfunctioning computer systems are holding Thraesians hostage in their homes, offices and transporters."

Croix watched somberly as a handful of hopeful people still stood amidst the rubble by the Gates, waiting for their loved ones to return.

"The Consortium is refusing to open the Passage Gates. They argue it is too dangerous with a level-five invasion of the Net underway," said Hotma.

"But the Chosen can't wait another eleven years," interjected Croix. "That's an additional forty-four Thrae years. They'll age and die the 'oment they cross the Gates."

"'Ve know," said Hotma, regretfully. "NetWatch is doing everything they can. But the Consortium is adamant. If they open the Gates and the Viruses gain access to Cygnus X-5, there is no stopping the Meta-hackers from ruling our Universe and pillaging Thrae."

Croix looked down. He knew this meant a lifetime for him in the Underground.

Netman squeezed Croix's shoulder reassuringly. "Hotma, you tell NetWatch that we'll put BeelzeButt and his men on ice before the Passage Gates open. The Chosen are going home!"

The transmission began to cut out as images of Didgit, chained to a wall in a dark tomb, filled the screen. An operating table sat ominously in the center of the room with several sharp electronic instruments on a nearby cart.

"What has BeelzeButt done to her?" demanded Netman.

"Nothing, yet," answered Hotma as the audio weakened. "But BeelzeButt sent you a message. He wants you to bring the boy to the Matrix at 23:55 if you want to see Didgit again." The transmission went dead.

Fifteen

OPERATION SNOWSHOE

The NetShuttle was approaching Volan CF1, known as the Matrix. Croix and the twins sat with their heads pressed against the shuttle flight deck window, mesmerized by the brilliance of the glowing white moon that pierced the blackness of Cyberspace.

Volan CF1 was a glacier moon covered with ice and snow. Its jagged mountain peaks and sub-zero climate made it nearly impossible to inhabit. Because of its harsh environment and remote location, the Net chose Volan to store its most precious resource, the Servers. A camp had been built in the enormous crater at the top of Volan Mountain, the highest peak in all of the Net. The crater, formed fifty thousand years ago by a nickel and iron meteorite that had slammed into the mountaintop, measured five miles across and two miles deep. Nestled within the crater walls, and thus shielded from the elements, was the Matrix—a village of massive observatory—like titanium dome structures, each towering six-hundred-feet high and nearly three-hundred-feet wide—housing the Net's thousands of precious Servers behind high-security steel walls.

Unbeknownst to anyone but Netman, one native civilization thrived on Volan—the Snowshoe people. They were mysterious but benevolent life forms who dwelled in the frozen tundra. Small white creatures with snowshoe-shaped feet, the Snowshoes spent their waking days mining under the snow for precious minerals and elements to feed them during their ten-year hibernation period. Their elaborate underground tunnels ran hundreds of miles in all directions. Although they didn't know it yet, Netman was counting on the Snowshoes to help him capture BeelzeButt and put an end to his Cybergalactic war.

"We'll be arriving in less than thirty minutes," reported Iso. Netman glanced at his watch: It was 22:00. "Good," replied Netman. "We should beat BeelzeButt and have time to start the evacuation."

"What evacuation?" asked Ram.

"Let's suit up and I'll fill you in."

Iso stayed on deck while the others followed Netman below. Netman threw open the doors to the weapons room, housing all the Netgadgetry, Netporters, armor and weapons stocked from the Hideout. "Hurry. We don't have much time."

Netman took Croix over to a special locker and pulled out his gear: a white racing helmet decorated with black lightning, matching body armor, protective black knee boots, a silicon full-body shell, extrasensory goggles and black gloves. The helmet featured a Backnose Propulsion System design for added speed. Scrawled on the black bill that jutted out from the top of the helmet and across the body armor was the word, "Netman."

"The helmets are wired for communication, and the gloves are equipped with lethal lasers if you need them," said Netman. "Krash and

Burn will show you how to operate them. Are you sure you want to do this?" asked Netman. "You can stay on the ship. You'll be safe here."

Croix nodded as he fingered the emerald stone around his neck. "No, I'm going," he said with certainty.

"Then there's one last thing," Netman said, opening the locker door wide. Written on the inside of the door in big black letters were the words "NO FEAR."

"We all have special gifts and powers, including you," said Netman. "But there is one thing at the heart of any true warrior, and it's fearlessness," said Netman, pointing to the words. "You have to believe in yourself. If you doubt—if you fear—you're dead. It doesn't matter what is going on in the outside world. It doesn't matter how many or how few are fighting against you or alongside you. If you believe in yourself, there's no stopping you. But the moment you let the outside world influence how you think of yourself, you're finished."

Netman handed Croix his gear. "Forget where you came from. You are of Anatares blood and destined to be a great warrior."

Croix smiled, his eyes twinkling at the thought.

Suited up in their multicolored gear, Netman walked the entire group through the plan in the war room. "When we arrive, we will split up. Croix, Payor and I will rescue Didgit and lure BeelzeButt and his men to the Matrix exactly at midnight. The rest of you will head directly to the Matrix and evacuate all the Servers into the Snowshoe tunnels. I will arrange for a small group of Snowshoes to meet you at the Matrix at 23:30 and escort the Servers to the tunnels. Meanwhile, Krash and Burn, you set up decoys in the domes to make it appear as if the Servers are all still there.

"At 24:00, when the VirusColony convenes at the Matrix, I'll make sure BeelzeButt and his men are dead center when the Snowshoes start the avalanche that will collapse the crater walls, burying BeelzeButt and the VirusColony under it, and creating the biggest DeepFreeze the Net has ever seen. Any questions?"

Ram sheepishly raised his hoof.

"Yes?" asked Netman.

"How do *we* get out?" asked Ram.

"Ah, good question. You! Your horns will airlift us out as the walls fall in," said Netman.

"That's quite a load," said Ram.

Iso nudged him encouragingly. "You can do it."

"Oh, no, here we go again," said Ram.

* * *

The NetShuttle hatch doors opened. Netman and the entire CyberSquad, including Iso, Croix and Payor, stepped out, suited in their extreme rocket-racing suits. They made an impressive group.

Croix looked out at Volan Mountain, with its gleaming ice cap that gave the mountain its shining summit. The ice cap was a thirty-seven square mile surface that smoothed and concealed all but the most rugged peaks and ridges. Its dazzling whiteness reflected the brilliant clouds that swept across its peak. The view was breathtaking. Croix had never seen such beauty.

Although it was now almost 22:30, it was still daylight. The sun never set on Volan. Everything was distorted on the moon because of its rotation on the Net. They were lucky it was only thirty below zero.

Netman punched a key on his XK3 Netwatch. A platform beneath the belly of the shuttle lowered, revealing seven wicked-looking turbo BacknoseBlasters—high-speed, streamlined two-seater transporters designed for icy terrain. Netman and the CyberSquad started their Blasters. They elevated, revealing spike-studded rubber conveyor belts that ripped into the ice and snow for traction, and carving skis that enabled quick turns. Netman tested the LaserBlasters that were concealed in the head-lights on his machine's sleek, tapered front end. Satisfied, he turned to Croix and asked, "Do you really think Payor can help us track BeelzeButt?"

"Absolutely," responded Croix. "He's raring to go."

On cue, Payor jumped on with Croix and sniffed the air in all directions while Netman scanned the horizon with his Bionetculars. Payor caught a scent of something as the wind blew up from the east. He growled, pointing his snout in that direction.

"All right, we'll give it a shot," said Netman, snapping on his extrasensory goggles over his helmet. Netman revved his engine, yelling over the noise, "Let's go kick some Virusbutt!"

* * *

Hearing the lock turn, Didgit wriggled herself up along the dungeon wall. She could feel the slimy fungus growing along the windowless walls and she was nauseated from the disgusting odor in the air. Her wrists and hands were numb from the restraints. She was still groggy from the injections they had been giving her every two hours.

The doors opened and light streamed in, revealing the source of the stench: beneath the grill under her feet was a pool of red water, filled with floating pieces of rotted flesh from experiments gone awry, half-eaten meals and "accidents."

Lip entered carrying a restraint jacket and neck collar attached to foot harnesses. Didgit tried to get her bearings but she was so dizzy she could barely stand.

"We've landed. You are being moved to more luxurious quarters," announced Lip, releasing her arm restraints. Didgit's arms flopped to her sides, useless. The blood began pumping back into her limbs. "We plugged your nose so don't try using any of your gas on me." He fastened the heavy jacket around her body.

"Can't you wait before you put that thing on me? I can barely feel my arms," she said.

Ignoring her, he proceeded. "My heart breaks for you. You're lucky BeelzeButt didn't dump you below," said Lip, motioning to the grill. "That's where the enemy usually goes to rest in peace. We have some very hungry friends down there." At that moment, a sizable jagged-toothed jaw broke the surface and submerged with a floating arm.

"We recycle here," said Lip.

"How progressive," said Didgit, turning away. She made out the table in the far corner of the room. "Are we operating?" she asked.

"Not here. We're moving you to a more sophisticated lab," said Lip.

"Do I have a specific ailment?"

Fastening her neck restraints, he whispered excitedly, "We're taking your code! Now the Consortium can never stop us. We'll know how to disarm their secret weapon. The best part is, BeelzeButt's turning you into one of us, and you're going to kill Netman."

"Like that's going to happen," said Didgit, goading him.

Lip fastened the remaining restraints. "You won't have a choice. You'll be under our control. When we swap you for the boy, Netman will think that he got you, but instead he will have gotten BeelzeButt's maiden. BeelzeButt makes a great bedfellow, if you don't mind the noxious gas."

"Time for your medicine, my fair lady," announced BeelzeButt, entering. "It won't be long now before you're mine."

"You call that a plan!" said Didgit derisively. "Netman will know you modified my code."

BeelzeButt looked at Lip menacingly. "What have you been telling her?!"

"Nothing BZ," said Lip, cowering, "I didn't say anything."

"And I'll make sure you never do." BeelzeButt pushed a lever and the grill under Lip's feet dropped, sending him plunging thirty feet down into the hungry jaws below. His screams were muffled as the creature immediately pulled him under.

"Now, what were you saying?" asked BeelzeButt innocently.

"You don't scare me."

"I know. I love that about you. We're going to have a grand time together," said BeelzeButt, pulling out a vial of red maggots, slithering in black sludge. "I'm only sorry I won't be around long enough to spend more time with you."

"Traveling?" asked Didgit.

"You could say that. I'm setting up shop on Thrae. If you behave, maybe I'll send for you."

"Before or after you infect me?"

"After, of course." BeelzeButt held up vial. "You know what this is?"

"VirusSeed," said Didgit.

"This isn't just any seed, it's my seed—the most lethal seed on the Net. Soon, you'll be mine forever!" said BeelzeButt, pulling a syringe from his coat and injecting her in the arm. Didgit's eyes rolled back into her head as she passed out. Implant entered and noticed Lip's jacket floating in the pit below. "You called, sir?" he said, hiding his anger.

"Take her to the lab and prepare it for the procedure." Implant grabbed Didgit. He glanced painfully at the pit below, exiting.

"Implant," called BeelzeButt. Implant popped his head back in. "Don't get any ideas, or you'll be next."

* * *

Netman walked out of the blue ice cave talking to the leader of the Snowshoe delegation, Nevv, a charming all-white creature with brilliant blue eyes nestled into flaps on either side of his wide, friendly face. Standing three-feet tall, he was all legs, but his youthful enthusiasm was contagious.

"Don't worry, we'll bury 'em. We hate those Virus guys, especially that nasty BigButt," said Nevv.

"I appreciate your help," said Netman.

"Hey, anytime. You're the man. We were wondering if you were ever gonna come back."

"I was in the shop. Thanks again," said Netman, walking off and waving back to the full Snowshoe delegation. Croix watched, waiting patiently with Payor on the BacknoseBlaster.

"What did they say?" he asked excitedly.

"They agreed. It's all set to go at exactly midnight." Netman started his Blaster, adding, "They told me BeelzeButt landed just three miles from here over that ridge. You've got a pretty good nose for a Crog, Payor. Maybe we'll keep you around."

Payor barked happily at the thought.

"Now remember," warned Netman, "I don't want you anywhere near that place when I go in. I want you to wait outside for my signal. If anything goes wrong, blast back to the Matrix."

"Got it," said Croix starting his engine and putting on his gear. He reached into his pocket to get his gloves and discovered the balls that he had taken from the basket on BeelzeButt's transporter. He smiled and pushed them back into his pocket.

"All right, let's go," said Netman, blasting off.

***

The clock on the wall of the elaborate operating room read 23:25. "We don't have much time," said BeelzeButt to Leper. Didgit lay unconscious on the table, her head in a vicelike contraption, tubes running into her arms, backnose and mouth. "Now, you're sure you know how to remove the code intact, so we can decode it and use it against them?" asked BeelzeButt.

"Trust me," said Leper, slapping on his goggles and struggling to start the bulky saw. "Do I look like an amateur?"

"Yes."

Leper finally managed to maneuver the loud contraption over her head and locked it in place. He carefully lowered the spinning blade, slicing through her ponytail. He was just inches from her cranium when the window exploded.

"STOP!" yelled Netman, crashing into the room. The two were stunned. Netman pointed his CyberRayGun at BeelzeButt and yelled at Leper, "Shut it off and move away from the table. NOW! Or BigButt is history." BeelzeButt nodded for Leper to follow orders. Leper shut off the machine and backed up slowly.

"Netman, I'm impressed," said BeelzeButt. "How did you find me?"

Jamming a titanium cork into BeelzeButt's ButtHole to plug any viral leaks, he answered, "I did a little sniffing."

Payor lost his balance and fell through the window.

BeelzeButt roared, "You traitor. After all I did for you!" Payor growled with delight.

"Payor, tie them up," ordered Netman.

Payor eagerly ran over and using his jaws, tightly clamped the Netshackles around their hands and feet.

BeelzeButt winced. "You'll never get out alive, Netman. My men will kill you," said BeelzeButt.

"That's why you're coming with us. Anything happens to us, and you're on ice."

Netman unhooked Didgit and picked her up. He noticed the chopped ponytail and grabbed it. "Oh, she's going to be real mad. Now, move it."

Netman motioned for them to exit. Netman and Payor walked directly behind BeelzeButt and Leper, Netman's gun pointed at BeelzeButt's head.

As they headed down the hall, Implant and MoonRat came around the corner. They immediately raised their lasers. "Put them down!" ordered BeelzeButt. They obeyed.

"Get in line," ordered Netman. BeelzeButt nodded for them to comply. Implant and MoonRat reluctantly joined the procession.

"You know," said BeelzeButt to Netman as they neared the building's exit, "it's not too late for us to join forces. Together we could rule the Net."

"Don't you mean Thrae?"

BeelzeButt stared at him, dumbfounded.

"The boy overheard everything. Too bad he'll be going home without you," said Netman. Stepping through the exterior doors, Netman pushed the standing guard out of the way. Puppet, completely paralyzed by the BluHare oil's effects, fell face-first into the snow. "Maybe you'd like to say goodbye." Netman motioned to Croix in the distance, who waved on cue.

BeelzeButt fumed. "I'll get you for this!" he yelled as Netman sealed them in a storage bunker outside. Netman quickly threw Didgit on the BacknoseBlaster as BeelzeButt and the others rammed the door. "Get on!" yelled Netman to Payor. "The door and shackles won't hold." Payor jumped on behind Netman and held on tight as Netman blasted off.

Netman raced up to Croix, handing off Payor just as BeelzeButt and the others burst out of the bunker. "Perfect timing," said Netman, looking back. "Let's go." They revved their engines and took off.

BeelzeButt, Implant, MoonRat and Leper threw on their fierce-looking Virus headgear with the "ButtMen" insignia on the front and tore after them on their nasty ButtBlasters.

Didgit began to stir as the wind whipped against her face. She turned, relieved to see Netman and said, "Thank God, it's you. He was planning on taking me as his mate. Can you imagine a more horrifying death?"

"Well, he's hot on our trail, so don't count him out yet," said Netman. Didgit looked back and saw the four were gaining on them. "What are you waiting for, step on it!"

"Hang on," said Netman, flying over a cornice, dropping twenty feet onto a steep slope. Netman checked his mirror. Croix flew off the cornice right behind him, landing a bit unsteadily but managing to right himself. Payor barely managed to stay on. One by one, BeelzeButt and the others flew over the ledge, landing easily on the icy slope.

"What are we doing exactly? Why didn't you just kill him back there?" asked Didgit, holding on for dear life as they bounced down a slope of moguls.

"I need him to lure the Virus Colony into the Matrix. You know, I try to help you out, and this is the thanks I get."

"OK! Thank you!" she yelled over the loud motor as they jumped all over the slope.

Netman could see BeelzeButt gaining on Croix. He checked his watch. 23:56. He had four minutes before the Viruses were going to blow the Matrix. Netman slowed down to allow Croix to catch up. Within seconds, the five BacknoseBlasters were racing in tandem. BeelzeButt was trying to run Croix off the course. A corkscrew-shaped drill came out of a side slot on BeelzeButt's ButtBlaster and drilled along Croix's Blaster. Croix moved his leg just in time, but the massive drill sliced open his left engine. He started losing speed.

Netman could see the crater on the horizon. They were close. He whipped around a quick turn, taking them into a dense alpine forest, hoping to slow BeelzeButt down. Coming around the bend, MoonRat lost control and impaled himself on a tree. Croix's motor started to sputter.

"Hang on, Croix!" yelled Netman. "We're almost there. Use your auxiliary power." Croix desperately searched the gauges for auxiliary. Krash hadn't shown him that. He started to panic. He couldn't find it. Payor growled as BeelzeButt pulled up beside them. He heard the familiar ShadowVirus voice in his head, chanting, "You're a dead man!" He tried to shake it, remembering what Netman had said.

Suddenly, Payor nosed Croix's shoulder and pointed to Netman, racing ahead for what looked like a sheer cliff. BeelzeButt pulled up. Croix managed to accelerate, but BeelzeButt fired his laser blaster, hitting him right in the chest with such force it knocked him back into Payor. Croix looked down at his chest and realized the stone that hung from his neck had taken the hit and saved his life.

Didgit, straddled backward on Netman's rocket, fired her CyberRayGun over Netman's shoulder and nailed BeelzeButt's engine, igniting it.

"Yeah!" she yelled, raising her hand triumphantly. Then she noticed her hair.

"Looking for this?" asked Netman, whipping out her hair. The blood drained from her face.

"It was him, not me." Netman yelled, shielding himself from Didgit.

"I'm going to kill you!" she screamed at BeelzeButt.

"Hang on!" yelled Netman as he jumped off the cliff, crashing down the vertical crater wall. Croix followed with renewed vigor while Payor held on tight. They miraculously landed. Croix was relieved to see the domes below. Standing alone along the ridge of the crater, the VirusColony waited with the XRS ready to go. They looked out, confused, as Netman and Croix flew over the ridge with BeelzeButt in close pursuit, his engine ablaze and sputtering.

Although perplexed, the VirusColony moved in. Standing across the ridge, Gargoyle, the ChickenChoker and a few other Viruses observed the chaos below. "I recognize that nose, that's Netman!" yelled the ChickenChoker. "That's it, we're out of here," ordered Gargoyle.

Suddenly, Croix's left engine died out. Implant pulled up and tried to pull Croix off the Blaster, but Payor bit into him, ripping off one of his many arms. Implant screamed, losing control of the Blaster and flipped uncontrollably down the crater, taking out Leper before they crashed in a fiery heap at the base.

Startled by the explosion, BeastBomber ordered, "Load the XRS!" The deadly explosive ammunition, three black balls identical to the two Croix carried, was loaded into the weapon.

Huddled inside the main door of the central server dome, Iso and the others watched the clock as it turned to 23:59. Iso ordered, "Let's go!" and burst through the door with his CyberRayGun blasting.

Netman and Didgit skidded into camp on their Blasters, followed by Croix and BeelzeButt. The Viruses weren't sure what was going on. Before Croix could stop his Blaster, BeelzeButt leapt off his and tackled Croix to the ground. The Viruses pointed the XRS at Netman and the CyberSquad. They raised their hands in defeat.

BeelzeButt wrestled Croix up, kicking and screaming. Payor lay helplessly, wedged under the weight of the overturned Blaster.

"Looks like the Net will be mine after all," said BeelzeButt triumphantly to Netman.

"You mean Thrae. Have you told the VirusColony of your plan to infect the boy, so when he returns to Thrae tonight you'll go with him?" asked Netman. The Viruses looked at each other, murmurs rippling through the crowd.

Croix suddenly noticed the ammunition balls that were being loaded into the XRS.

"Fry 'em," ordered BeelzeButt. No one moved.

"Did you tell them how you were planning on double-crossing them?" continued Netman. "While they got to rule the small Net moons, you'd get all of Thrae?"

The Viruses turned suspiciously to BeelzeButt, awaiting an answer.

"He's lying!" shouted BeelzeButt, turning to the crowd.

Taking advantage of the diversion, Croix broke free and ran. He took the two balls out of his pocket and yelled, "Catch!" to BeelzeButt as he threw them straight up in the air.

BeelzeButt's mouth dropped as the balls flew through the air. The Viruses held their breath as BeelzeButt ran to catch one, then dove for the other.

Suddenly, the earth began to shake. The crater walls were disintegrating right in front of them. "Avalanche!" screamed the Viruses, running.

Croix pulled Payor out from under the Blaster. They ran to join the others as the crater collapsed. Viruses were drowning in cascading ice and snow. BeelzeButt turned hearing the chilling sound of the glacier floor crack beneath him. It suddenly opened up, sending hundreds of Viruses careening down its 500-foot-deep ravine. BeelzeButt dropped, but caught the side of the glacier, his nails digging into the ice. He desperately tried to hang on as Netman approached.

"Going down?" asked Netman, lending him a hand. Plummeting to his icy death, BeelzeButt screamed, "I'll get you for this!"

With the crater crumbling around them, Ram screamed, "HOLD ON!" over the thunderous noise. The group grabbed onto him as he blasted them straight out of the Matrix just as the remaining walls gave way and collapsed, burying the VirusColony in the biggest DeepFreeze the Galaxy had ever seen.

Sixteen

THE SCORPION PRINCE

The NetShuttle zoomed into the NorthCity at exactly 00:50. They had ten minutes before the Passage Gates closed.

Netman and the CyberSquad raced through the streets with Croix and Payor in tow. The Net was a disaster area, but basic communication had been established with Thrae in time to communicate the news of BeelzeButt's demise, thus ensuring the opening of the Gates.

They got there with just minutes to spare. The grounds were mobbed, as thousands of people pushed and pulled to get through in time.

Croix leaned down to catch his breath. Payor stood by sadly, suddenly realizing he was about to lose his master.

"Croix, good luck," said Netman, shaking his hand. "I know you'll do great things for the Net on Thrae. Don't stop believing in the impossible." The group took turns hugging Croix goodbye.

Croix suddenly felt overcome with emotion. "I don't know what to say," he said humbly. "Thank you. I could never have made it without you."

"Your father would have been proud," said Netman.

Croix smiled, filled with mixed emotions.

"Tell NetWatch to send us some help," said Didgit teasingly. "We have a lot to do to put this place back together."

"You better go before they close the Gates," warned Netman. "Good luck and remember us when you log onto the Net up there. A whole army of people down here make that possible for you."

Croix smiled, knowing all too well. He petted a sad Payor one last time and waved goodbye, walking through the Gates as the clock struck 01:00.

* * *

It was a beautiful sunny day back on Thrae. "Here they come!" shouted Weldon from his office window. Twiggy, Gopher, Scooter and Piper ran in. They watched as the giant boulder at the base of Deadwood Mountain began to shake, marking the opening of the Passage Gates.

The boulder rolled out as if pushed by an invisible force, revealing the secret dark tunnel behind it, the Passageway. In seconds, the Chosen flooded out into the bright, warm light. The large awaiting crowd glee-fully embraced their suddenly aged loved ones as they streamed onto the field. They were shocked to see the grounds covered in rubble and debris from the violent earthquakes wrought by the Meta-hackers' reign of terror.

"It's certainly not what they were expecting," said Twiggy.

"No. But at least they're home," said Weldon.

"Netman rocks!" said Scooter, high-fiving Piper.

"Just wait until we download our new RocketBoard features to their Hideout," said Scooter.

"Forget it. Come check out the beastly Netman MonsterTruck I've got cooking," said Piper, walking out with him.

"Glad to see some things don't change," said Gopher, calling after them. "We have lots of work to do! The Net's a mess."

Weldon and Twiggy headed down the escalator to greet the Chosen. "So what do you think?" asked Weldon.

"I think we got lucky," said Twiggy, smiling.

His father's portrait caught Weldon's eye as they descended into the lobby. "Luck had nothing to do with it," said Weldon glancing back at his father's likeness. "Nothing at all."

* * *

Netman and the CyberSquad walked slowly down the hill with a dejected Payor lagging behind. As they reached the bottom of the hill, Netman heard someone call, "Netman! Wait!"

He turned and saw Croix running after them. Payor bolted up the hill, practically knocking Croix over in his excitement.

"What happened?" asked Netman, catching up.

"I turned back. I realized this is my home. There is nothing for me on Thrae; my family is here. I want to go back to the Underground and help rebuild it, make it a decent place to live for the Netpeople who have to serve there."

Netman looked silently at the others. "Are you sure?" he asked.

"Yes," said Croix firmly.

"Very well," said Netman. "Do you have your sword?" "

Croix nodded, handing it over to him.

"Please kneel," said Netman. Croix knelt before him lowering his head, unsure of what Netman was about to do.

"I hereby christen you 'The Scorpion Prince,' ruler and protector of the Underground. All that came before is history. All that is to come is your great destiny. Go and fulfill it," said Netman, christening Croix with the glistening sword by touching it to each of his shoulders.

"Rise," said Netman.

Croix stood, feeling electric.

"You'll need help."

"I have it," said Croix, patting Payor on the head. "But you'll need a new title, too. We can't have you going through life with a name like 'Pet At Your Own Risk.'"

Payor barked in agreement.

Croix raised his sword. "I hereby christen you 'Colgate,' keeper of the Underground," said Croix, touching each of Colgate's shoulders with his sword as Netman had done to him.

Colgate beamed, wagging his tail with excitement. He was a new Crog.

"I think this calls for a celebration," said Netman.

"I know the perfect place on Cray, best service in town," said Iso.

"To Cray!" they cheered as they disappeared down the hill.

THE END

Epilogue

"Step right up," called the PageBoss to the long line of anxiously awaiting PageBoys. "No pushing. There's plenty of time to get your private viewing. Have your Nash ready, sorry no Nedit Nards."

The PageBoss dramatically pulled back the tent's red velvet curtain, announcing, "It is my pleasure to present the renowned Mr. Red."

Reclining on a bed of sumptuous pillows and surrounded by attendants, a regal looking Red nodded at the boys.

The group of PageBoys hustled in, clutching their new copies of the best selling E-Book, *I Used to Be Just Another Netschmuk.*

"Could I have your autograph, Mr. Red?" asked one.

"Why, of course," said Red, reaching grandly for his E-Book.

Another Pageboy, pointing to the shrine in the far corner, asked with great reverence, "Is that it?"

"Be careful," said Red, motioning to an attendant to escort them.

There, in a darkened corner, illuminated by a single spotlight, was a cordoned-off glass case that housed the priceless Netman autograph.

"Wow!" exclaimed one, leaning over the ropes to get a closer look at Netman's signature that was scrawled on top of the wrinkled "Secret Trails to Netman's Hideout" map.

"Is that for real?" exclaimed one PageBoy in awe.

"Sure is," said Red, proudly

"How did you do it?" asked another.

"Anything's possible," said Red, winking, "if you believe."

About the Author

Fernanda Carapinha Erlanger was born in Portugal and grew up in Massachusetts. She spent many years working in the entertainment industry and was involved in the development of numerous televison series. Fernanda lives in Malibu, California with her husband, Phil, and their two labs, Boomer and Lola. This is her first novel.

Visit Netman on the Web at:
www.netmanworld.com

• •